"You want to fight me, Addison?"

"Very much so." Addison's eyes were wide, dark. Excitement lit her cheeks.

Logan rubbed his thumb over her ankle, tracing the delicate bone in circles. "What's the wager?"

"Full control for the next three days. If I win, you'll fix up my apartment and then leave me to my business unless I ask for your protection." She folded her hands neatly on the table. "And you have to tell everyone at work that I'm a better boss than you are."

A smile twitched on his lips. "And if I win?"

"You can boss me around as much as you like. I'll do anything you want without complaint."

Her words rocketed through him, scorching him from the inside out. "Anything?"

"Whatever your wicked heart desires."

Dear Reader,

I've had my share of jobs over the years: ice cream server, sales assistant, makeup artist, human resources officer, training facilitator, communications consultant, author. One of my jobs involved working in a cybercrime and information-security environment. At the time I knew nothing about it.

But over the years I learned so much—how people could steal your identity, how catfishing and social engineering worked, how people could hack into your phone or computer. As someone who was always better with words than technology, all this information fascinated me.

When I had the chance to put some of it into a book, I was thrilled. And who better to go up against a cyberstalker hell-bent on revenge than Logan Dane? You might remember Logan from the previous Dangerous Bachelors Club books. He's the head of Cobalt & Dane Security alongside the heroine, Addison Cobalt.

Logan and Addi have an interesting relationship. They've always battled for attention and respect, then later for the "top dog" position at Cobalt & Dane. This has created a not-so-healthy competition between them. But when someone targets Addison, they must work together to track down the stalker's identity before Logan loses Addison for good.

I really hope you enjoy Logan and Addison's story. You can find out what's coming next by checking out my website, stefanie-london.com, or Facebook, Facebook.com/stefanielondonauthor. I love chatting to readers, so feel free to drop me a line anytime.

With love,

Stefanie

Stefanie London

———

Mr. Dangerously Sexy

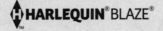
HARLEQUIN® BLAZE®

Recycling programs
for this product may
not exist in your area.

ISBN-13: 978-0-373-79954-1

Mr. Dangerously Sexy

Copyright © 2017 by Stefanie Little

Printed in U.S.A.

USA TODAY bestselling author **Stefanie London** is a voracious reader who has dreamed of being an author her whole life. After sneaking several English-lit subjects into her "very practical" business degree, she got a job in corporate communications. But it wasn't long before she turned to romance fiction. She recently left her hometown of Melbourne to start a new adventure in Toronto and now spends her days writing contemporary romances with humor, heat and heart.

For more information on Stefanie and her books, check out her website at stefanie-london.com or her Facebook page at Facebook.com/stefanielondonauthor.

Books by Stefanie London

Harlequin Blaze

The Dangerous Bachelors Club

A Dangerously Sexy Christmas
A Dangerously Sexy Affair
A Dangerously Sexy Secret

Harlequin Kiss

Breaking the Bro Code
Only the Brave Try Ballet

Harlequin Presents

The Tycoon's Stowaway

To get the inside scoop on Harlequin Blaze and its talented writers, visit Facebook.com/BlazeAuthors.

All backlist available in ebook format.

Visit the Author Profile page at Harlequin.com for more titles.

To my fellow Blaze Babes, it's been a blast.

1

ADDISON COBALT'S FATHER had made a living out of taking down bad guys, so she knew the world had an ugly underbelly. But knowing it and experiencing it were two different things. She smoothed her hands over the printed email that sat on her desk. Hateful words stared up at her.

"I don't understand what's going on here," she said, furrowing her brow.

Rhys Glover, the IT manager for Cobalt & Dane Security, pursed his lips. "He's threatening you."

"Yes, I got that from the 'I'm going to kill you' section of this email. But I don't know who could have sent it or *why*. I don't have any enemies."

"Clearly, you do."

Raking a lacquered red nail down the neat rows of twelve-point print, she searched for a clue as to the identity of the anonymous email sender. "You'd think that if he was going to threaten my life, he could at least introduce himself first."

Rhys narrowed his dark eyes. "You don't seem to be taking this very seriously, Addi."

One of Rhys's staff members had come across the email

that morning when she'd been combing through the spam filter on an unrelated assignment. She'd brought it directly to Rhys. The message had never made it to Addison's email address because of its excessive profanity.

"I'm not sure how anyone could take an email seriously from someone who calls themselves 'your worst nightmare.' I mean, how clichéd is that?" She rolled her eyes. "Thanks for bringing this to me, but it's probably a hoax. Just some guy who hates women and wants to get his jollies by sending a nasty email. I'm not too worried—"

"I think we should involve Logan."

Addison bristled. "He has bigger things to worry about than some misogynistic idiot."

Truth was, she didn't want Logan getting involved. She tried to keep anything remotely personal as far away from him as possible. Their relationship was strictly business, and it had to stay that way. It was bad enough that she had to accept that everyone viewed *him* as the boss despite their being equal partners, and she'd rather stab herself in the eye with her own stiletto before admitting she needed his help.

Besides, there was the issue of her top secret plans to start her own business separate from Cobalt & Dane. Having Logan stick his nose into her personal life wasn't something that she could allow at the moment.

"The safety and well-being of everyone in this company *is* his responsibility." Rhys ran a hand over his cropped dark hair.

"*Our* responsibility," she corrected. "Since my name is on the wall here, his responsibilities are also mine."

"You know what I mean. This is Logan's bread and butter, not yours."

Like she needed the reminder. "That might be true, but I'm still your boss."

"Are you telling me not to say anything to him?" Rhys shook his head. "I'm not comfortable—"

"That's exactly what I'm saying." She scanned the email again. "Whoever this person is, they haven't made a move. This email was sent two days ago and I haven't had any strange phone calls or anyone stopping me in the street. It's a load of crap."

"The things he says are pretty specific."

"Precisely my point. If he were planning to execute any of this, why wouldn't he keep his mouth shut instead of leaving a happy little trail of evidence like some kind of deranged version of *Hansel and Gretel*?" She shrugged. "Now, security might not be my 'bread and butter,' but that seems a little odd to me."

Rhys made a noncommittal noise. "Better safe than sorry."

"I *am* safe. My apartment is totally secure, as are the offices here. I appreciate the concern, Rhys, but I'm fine."

Addison drummed her nails against the surface of the desk. She wouldn't admit it to Rhys—or anyone—but the email *had* shaken her a little. It was so angry. So vitriolic.

But if there was one thing she knew for certain, it was that people were much braver in front of a computer screen than they were in real life. Addison was an active participant in several women-in-business groups. She'd seen firsthand the kind of crap people posted online, but she'd bet her last dollar bill that none of them would have the guts to say those things to her face. So she didn't put much stock in this email.

And she certainly wouldn't subject herself to asking Logan freaking Dane for help.

"You're not worried?"

She shook her head. "This is just some weak little person sitting high and mighty behind his keyboard trying to get his thrills by scaring a woman who dares to be in a position of power. I'm not falling for it."

"I still think we should tell Logan."

"Rhys, I promise if anything else seems out of the ordinary I'll bring it up with him." She folded the email in two and tucked it into her organizer. "But we've got the leadership retreat starting on Monday and I have a ton of stuff to do in preparation. *And* I want Logan's eye on the prize with this strategy stuff. He'll do anything to get out of it. Don't give him the distraction."

"I *really* don't feel comfortable sitting on this," Rhys said.

"I don't care." Addison stood and made a shooing motion with her hands. "Now, get out of here and don't stay late. You should be spending the weekend with that lovely woman of yours. If she stops sending brownies into the office, the staff will have my hide."

"Fine." Rhys pushed up from the chair on the other side of her desk and went to leave. "But promise me you'll let one of us know the second you see anything odd. Okay?"

"Cross my heart and hope to die," she replied, making a cross over her chest with her finger. "Now get out of here."

She smiled to herself as Rhys left. Her IT manager was a great guy, if a little too uptight in her opinion. But once he was gone, a feeling of unease developed in her chest. Surveying her office, she tried to shake it off.

It's nerves about the retreat, that's all.

The Cobalt & Dane management team would be spending three days in Addison's cottage in upstate New York assessing their progress against the business strategy they'd developed six months ago. It was also an excuse to get the team together to socialize, which they were often too busy to do. But despite their crazy workload, the team was small and tight-knit. Addison's father had always cultivated a close bond with his team back when he first started the company. She'd made it her mission to keep that legacy alive.

Except now she wanted to leave her father's company and strike out on her own. Completely on her own... well, except for taking a few key staff members with her.

It wasn't just that Logan was viewed as the boss over her, but in a company that dealt with security she was out of her element with the subject matter. The thing was, Addison took care of *everything* that wasn't security. That included finances, human resources, payroll, training, business development, internal communications, etc. The list went on and on. At times her lack of security knowledge worked to her advantage because she was unbiased and could offer a fresh perspective that hadn't been colored by bad assignments.

But despite her valuable input and the fact that she was the one who kept the lights on by ensuring the company paid its bills and its employees, she was still seen as the number two. That wasn't going to change; she'd never be top dog here.

Worse still, she'd never command the respect her father did. And for a girl who was competitive to the bone...that hurt.

Shaking off the negative thoughts, she brought her

attention back to the task at hand—preparing for the retreat. It had become her tradition to head up to the cottage the weekend before so that everything was ready to go for the Monday morning welcome session.

Her body relaxed in anticipation. A weekend alone at the cottage sounded like absolute bliss. She had a new book, a few bottles of her favorite wine and a swimsuit already packed. All she had to do was finish up at the office and then she could start the slow trudge out of Manhattan.

Scanning her list of things to bring from the office, she found the last item unchecked: the binder with all the notes from the last retreat, which sat neatly on the top shelf of her bookcase.

There were few things as precarious as trying to navigate a step stool in Louboutins, but Addison wasn't about to let OH&S get in the way of her love for a good pair of high heels. She climbed to the top of the stool, her fingers reaching for the thick binder. Of course, the one thing she needed was on the highest shelf. Wasn't that always the way?

"You know, I'm not sure I ever believed in heaven," a deep voice said. "But my dad always told me I'd find the answer to my questions if I looked up to God."

Logan Dane leaned against the door frame to his partner's office, a smirk tugging at his lips. Any chance to throw Addison off guard was not to be missed. Although truth be told, a chance to torture himself with the vision of her amazing legs was not to be missed, either.

"I've got good aim, Logan. Don't make me throw something at you."

Instead of coming down, she leaned farther forward,

causing her fitted pencil skirt to ride higher up the backs of her legs. His breath caught in his throat when a sliver of lace revealed that her stockings stopped midthigh. Sweet mother of all things holy.

Between the tight skirt, the black lace and the candy-red soles on her shoes, it was a picture fit for a dirty dream.

Yeah, 'cause the thing you need right now is another image of Addison to avoid fantasizing over. Don't you have enough guilt on your shoulders already?

"I'd like to see you try," he said.

She retrieved a binder and climbed down, making a show of smoothing out the wrinkles on her skirt. Her red nails matched the underside of her heels.

"Did you want something, Logan? Or are you just here to ogle my legs?"

He cleared his throat. "I wasn't—"

"Sure you weren't."

Busted. "I can't help it. You've got some damn fine pins."

Shaking her head, she bent down and picked up her bag from the floor. This time he kept his eyes away from her ass. Willpower, when he had it, was a wonderful thing.

"You all ready for the retreat on Monday?" she asked, ignoring his comment. "We've got an early start."

"Don't worry, I'll be on time."

"No, be early." She gathered up her organizer and slid it into her bag. "I'll need help setting up for the first session."

"Yes, ma'am. Anything else you want me to do, Miss Bossy Boots?" He walked into her office and placed his palms on her desk. "As if it isn't bad enough you'll be talking numbers at me all through the retreat."

"Just arrive in one piece." Her eyes flickered over him, sending a trail of heat straight from his chest to his groin. "I'm not sure what your weekend plans are, but I don't want you rolling up hungover and with lipstick on your collar."

He'd done that once, and she'd never let him live it down, though he absolutely deserved the censure. He hadn't been subtle when he'd started dating his ex. But he'd put a stop to that soon after—no more women, no more fooling around. Still, Addison had kept her distance ever since.

"I wouldn't let the staff see me in that state." He pressed his hand to his chest. "You know that."

"Oh right, to them you've got to be the Big Bad Wolf." She continued packing her bag without looking up, her long golden hair slipping over her shoulder to conceal her expression. "Lucky me, getting to see the real you."

He detected the slightest waver in her voice, undercutting the otherwise frosty tone. The show with his ex had been partly for Addison's benefit, though it was hard to keep reminding himself he'd done the right thing by them both. Knowing that he'd hurt her so badly made him feel like a bastard.

"You're one of the lucky few, Addi."

"I count my blessings," she said drily. "Anyway, I'm heading off early. Got to make a head start down to the cottage before this traffic gets insane."

"You sure you don't want a weekend guest?"

"Absolutely positively one hundred percent sure." A smile twitched on her lips, and his heartbeat kicked up a notch. "I'm going to sit in the hot tub until my hands turn to prunes. I'm going to drink wine and do yoga and be totally peaceful. No one is going to ruin that for me, especially not you."

"Message received."

Despite his best effort to keep his mind on the business retreat, a thought skittered through his brain like a pebble skipping over a pond. Was she the bikini type, or would she wear something more sophisticated in the hot tub? Black or white? Or something colorful?

Would it have one of those string tie-ups that could be easily loosened with a single—

"I *said* is there anything else you need before I go?" She hoisted her bag over one shoulder and picked up a box of supplies with *retreat* neatly printed on the side in black marker.

"Nope, I just came in here to wind you up."

She shook her head. "Now that's the first honest thing you've said to me all day."

"I said you had great pins," he corrected as he held the door for her. "I stand by that."

She muttered something under her breath as she walked past him, but he caught a rueful smile on her lips.

They had an odd relationship. But he'd take their strange mix of teasing and power struggles over not having her around any day. Addison was one of the few people who meant something to him.

Just remember that next time you get tempted to take a closer look at those pins, Dane. She's off-limits. One slip does not make it okay to go back for seconds.

Her tinkling laughter carried through the open-plan office as she stopped to say goodbye to her team. One of the young guys in accounts took the box from her hands and could barely keep his tongue in his mouth as he escorted her to the elevators. Logan's fists clenched instinctively.

Sure, he knew she was off-limits, but that didn't mean he could stand the thought of someone else touching her. Having her. He was all too familiar with how good she felt, how her body reacted to the barest touch. She was sensitive in the best way possible, and he'd given in to her all too easily once.

"Never again," he muttered under his breath, turning away from the sight of her and the young staff member before he said something he would regret. "She's not yours."

A few minutes later, Logan was knee-deep in work. Running Cobalt & Dane kept him busy, and Friday afternoons were no exception. Besides, Addison would have the team on a tight leash during the retreat next week, which meant he needed to be on top of things before finishing up for the weekend. He'd never quite understood the necessity of taking time off to discuss boring stuff like financials and recruiting strategy—surely that was a job for all those bean counters he'd hired at Addison's request.

A knock at his office door pulled him out of his thoughts.

"Logan?" Rhys leaned in, a wary expression on his face. "You got a second?"

"Sure." Logan motioned for him to enter. "What's going on?"

"I'm concerned about an email we received. I took it to Addison and she asked me not to bother you because of the retreat next week, but…"

Logan frowned. "But?"

"Here." Rhys slid a piece of paper across the table. "I think we need to be worried about this."

Logan scanned the email, his fingers gripping the paper tighter and tighter as he read until it crumpled under the pressure. His instinct was to lash out, to curse Addison and Rhys for not bringing this to him right away. But this was his fault. He knew why Addison didn't want him involved—and it wasn't because of the retreat. It was because he'd put distance between them and now she was teaching him a lesson.

"Have there been any other emails like this?" he asked, smoothing the paper down flat on his desk.

"Not that we've seen. I've put a flag on this email address so I'll know if he tries to contact anyone in the company from this point on." Rhys bobbed his head. "Addison isn't worried about this guy, but I don't think we can ignore him."

"You should have come to me first." Logan raked a hand through his hair.

The vile words glared up at him from the paper, the threats waving at him like giant red flags. How could Addison have thought this was nothing?

Because she'd rather prove herself to be independent than come to you for help.

"It's addressed to her, Logan. What would she have done if I took it you first?" He threw his hands up in the air. "I get that you two have this weird tug-of-war thing going on, but I'm sick of walking on eggshells around you two instead of doing my job."

"If you see anything else like this come in, you come to me. Got it?" He banged his fist down on the desk. "I don't care if the email says 'top fucking secret, for Addison's eyes only' in big bold letters."

Rhys sighed. "Fine. But you'll have to back me up when she flips out."

"If she's alive and well enough to be shouting, then I'm happy."

He'd promised Addison's father—the man who'd been his boss and his mentor—that he would always look out for her. That he would keep her safe from this crazy, screwed-up world they lived in. Only once had he broken that vow. One night two years ago, when his willpower had failed him and he'd given in to the desire he'd managed to keep at bay for almost a decade.

"I've got my team looking into the sender's details," Rhys said. "But I'm not sure how much we'll be able to turn up from a webmail account. People don't usually use their real details, especially if they're planning to send emails like this."

"Just find out whatever you can."

Rhys nodded. "You know she's going to be all by herself this weekend, right?"

"No, she's not." Logan folded the printed email up small enough to fit in his pocket. "Addison is going to have a guest at the cottage, whether she likes it or not."

2

ADDISON ROLLED HER shoulders as she settled in for the last leg of her journey. After driving for more than three hours, her muscles were desperate for a stretch, and she wanted something to eat that wasn't birdseed masquerading as an energy bar. Thankfully, it wouldn't be long until she reached her father's cottage on Cayuga Lake. Then she could reheat the lasagna she'd prepared last night and crack open a bottle of wine. Her stomach grumbled at the thought of a hot meal.

"Just a little farther," she said to her reflection in the rearview mirror. As if in response, her phone vibrated. "Again, Logan?"

He'd been calling every half hour or so since she'd made it through Newark. Despite ignoring him because her phone's hands-free unit wasn't hooked up, it had become clear he had a bee in his bonnet. That was Logan in a nutshell: dogged persistence.

Addison pulled over at a gas station and killed the engine so she could answer the phone. "Okay, crazy person. What's going on?"

"Where are you?"

She pushed the door open and got out of the car. The air was balmy with summer warmth and she took the opportunity to get the blood flowing through her limbs. "I'm on my way to the cottage."

"No, I mean specifically." There was an urgency in his voice that made the hairs on her arms stand on end.

She told him the name of the gas station as she walked through its doors. Bright, harsh lighting made her squint and she was hit with a chilly blast of air-conditioning. If Logan was going to hold her up, she may as well grab a drink.

"What's going on?" she asked as she opened the door to the refrigerator, stilling at the bellowing sound of a semi's horn on the other end of the line. "Are you on the road?"

Silence.

"Logan Matthew Dane, you better tell me what the hell is going on right now." She grabbed a Diet Coke and marched to the cashier. The man behind the counter eyed her warily as she handed the money over to him with what must have been a murderous look in her eyes. "If you intend on ruining my relaxing weekend I swear to God—"

"I saw the email."

She groaned. "Then tell Rhys he's fired. I mean it, turn around right now and go fire him."

"That might be difficult."

Addison wedged the phone between her ear and her shoulder so she could open her drink. "Why would that be difficult?"

"I'm already on the interstate."

Goddammit. "You're coming to the cottage?"

She walked out of the gas station, shaking her head.

If Logan showed up tonight she would send him straight back home. Or at the very least, to the nearest town. Spending the weekend alone with Logan Dane was *not* in her plans.

"I'll be there shortly," he said. "And don't take it out on Rhys. He did the right thing."

"So the right thing is not listening to his boss when she gives him a *direct* order?" She leaned against her car and tipped her drink up to her lips. "I know for damn sure you wouldn't let anyone pull that shit on you."

Another car had driven into the gas station, and the guy gave Addison a sleazy once-over as he filled the tank of his red truck. Grimacing, she turned away.

"That's beside the point. In this case, we need to take precautions." Logan sighed. "I realize this isn't what you had planned for the weekend. But the cottage is huge. You won't even know I'm there. Unless of course you think my presence is too strong for you to ignore…"

"Your *ego* is too strong for me to ignore."

"Ahh, come on. I'm looking out for you, Addi. I promised your dad—"

"I remember what you promised him. But you're all overreacting. There is no threat. That email was sent days ago, and if Rhys hadn't found it we'd be none the wiser." She screwed the cap back onto her drink. "And *I* would be about to enjoy a peaceful weekend without having you around to bug me."

"I won't apologize for being careful when it comes to your well-being."

She wanted to ask why he thought her well-being was his business. Or his responsibility. But she already knew the answer to that. Two years ago, during her father's final hospital visit—the cancer eating away at his frail body—he'd passed the baton for her protection over to Logan. It was bad enough that he'd chosen Logan to fill his shoes as the head of Cobalt & Dane, but he hadn't even trusted her to take care of herself.

"Don't go into the cottage until I get there," he added. "Wait in your car and keep the doors locked. I'm not far behind you."

Gritting her teeth, she ended the call and slid into the driver's seat. This weekend was going to be a freaking nightmare.

On the bright side, at least now she could count on Logan being at the retreat on time. A wicked smile curved on her lips. If he wanted to play protector all weekend, then she'd give him something productive to do. He hated spreadsheets with a passion, so she'd hand him some of the biannual forecasts to read. *That* should keep him busy.

She turned the engine over and flicked on her headlights. The sun had dropped significantly since she'd arrived at the gas station. It would be pitch-black soon, and the cottage would be dark. Secluded.

What if Logan and Rhys were right? A shiver raced the length of her spine.

"There's no stalker, just like there's no bogeyman," she reminded herself. "There's no zombies, no killer llamas, no Freddy Krueger and no…whatever the hell that thing was in *Donnie Darko*."

But the words didn't comfort her. A tiny seed of fear had been planted by the email, and now it was flourishing under Logan's paranoia. She tapped the lock button and with a *click*, all four doors secured her inside. Shaking her head, she cursed herself for letting Logan get to her.

As she pulled onto the empty road leading toward the cottage, her lights swept across the horizon. Tall trees rushed past her windows in a blur of deep green. Growing up, the cottage had been her happy place—a haven where she'd spent time with her father and did all the things his busy schedule ordinarily excluded. Like fishing, inspecting butterflies and making homemade pizza.

Lights flashed in her rearview mirror as a car drove up behind her, pulling her out of her memories. The high beams shone in her eyes, blurring her vision.

"Inconsiderate moron," she grumbled under her breath as she adjusted the mirror to redirect the glare.

The car behind her was close. Too close. Like one sneeze away from a rear-ender close.

"What the hell?" Addison glanced at her speedometer and confirmed that she was indeed driving at the limit. "Give a girl some space, would you? Jerk."

With one lane of traffic in each direction, she couldn't pull over to let the impatient person pass. But no cars appeared to be coming the other way, so why didn't they simply overtake her? She pressed the accelerator down to put some space between them, but the other driver ate up the distance in seconds. The vehicle looked high, maybe a truck of some kind. But the lights were so blindingly bright that she couldn't make out any specific details like color or model.

"Go around," she said, motioning with her hand for the driver to pass her.

She reached for her phone and hit redial on Logan's number. If he wasn't too far behind—as he'd said—then maybe he could get the plate number.

"Miss me already?" Logan's voice sounded far away on her phone's tiny speakers.

"Have you passed the gas station yet? There's this idiot tailgating me and I'm hoping you can get his plates." She pressed harder on the accelerator and glanced anxiously as the needle on the speedometer climbed higher. "He's making me nervous."

"I should be caught up to you soon, but I haven't passed the gas station yet. Drive carefully, okay?"

At that moment the truck pulled out beside her. "All good, looks like he's going to overtake me. About freaking time." She sighed. "No need to—"

A loud *crunch* cut her off and her car swerved violently. The gut-wrenching sound of metal on metal filled her ears and she had to yank the steering wheel to right the car. Her head snapped to the side in time to see the other vehicle coming back for seconds. She screamed. But it didn't make a lick of difference. Seconds later, her Audi hit dirt on the side of the road.

"Logan!" she cried out.

Another sickening *crunch* boomed and the car shook with impact. Then her headlights bounced around in front of her and she was flying over the gravel.

"ADDISON!" LOGAN YELLED through his phone, but the sound of squealing tires drowned him out. Her frightened scream cut into him. "Hang in there, Addi! I'm right behind you."

Except he wasn't. The road was dark and long and he wasn't exactly sure how much distance was between them.

"Logan, please—" Addison's terrified voice was cut short when the call died.

"Fuck!" he roared and planted his foot down on the accelerator.

The sides of the road weren't well illuminated and he *still* hadn't found the gas station. This was the usual route she took to the cottage—they'd driven it many times together. He was sure of it. But what if she'd gone another way tonight? What if she'd tried to find a short-cut or avoid the toll roads?

What if, what if, what if...

If something happened to her... God help him. He'd tear down every building in the state until he figured out who'd done this to her.

His car shot through the darkness, well over the limit. It didn't matter; nothing mattered except finding her. He eased off the gas as he rounded a corner.

"Come on, come on, come on," he chanted.

His eyes scanned the next stretch of road. Then a faint glow grew in the distance. Signs displaying the price per gallon appeared as he approached and he checked the name. Yes, this was it. The gas station she'd mentioned earlier. She shouldn't be too much farther along this road.

Pushing his car as hard as it would go, he reached for the glove compartment and flipped it open. His SIG P226 sat where he'd placed it earlier, the last resort he hoped never to need. But if anyone had brought harm to Addison, he wouldn't hesitate to use it.

The gas station whizzed past and darkness stretched out before him. Flicking on his high beams, he scanned the side of the road on both sides. Nothing.

"Come on, dammit." He slammed the steering wheel with the heel of his hand, tension tightening the muscles in his shoulders and arms. Making him ache. The blood drained from his knuckles, leaving them white.

His headlights brushed over the empty road and the

trees. At a curve ahead, a glint of something red caught his attention. The dot grew bigger. A truck.

Easing off the accelerator, his eyes scanned the area and sure enough, a trail of skid marks exited the road not too far up. He frantically searched for Addison's silver Audi, his heart in his mouth.

Her sporty little car wouldn't have been able to stand up to this much bigger vehicle. What if she'd...?

"Stop that right fucking now," he said to himself as he pulled over to the side of the road, a few feet behind the truck.

Freaking out wouldn't help anyone. If there was one thing he'd learned in his years of dealing with dangerous situations, it was that you had to stay cool, calm and collected. In control. No matter what horrors you might see.

He forced down the wash of dark worries and killed the engine. His fingers wrapped around his gun. The cold, hard steel of his SIG reassured him, helped him to slip into work mode. He knew the grip, knew the weight, knew how it would behave. And he let the familiarity soothe him.

Taking a deep breath, he flipped the safety off.

The night air was still around him when he stepped out of his car, as though the weather sensed that something was about to go down. Not even a breeze whispered past. Moving quietly, he peered farther down the side of the road. That's when he saw Addison's car.

The silver Audi was covered in brutal scratches. The metal of the back door had been pushed in. Her taillight was shattered. Thankfully, it appeared that she hadn't hit any of the trees that peppered the area. But the light from the road didn't extend far down the dip, and he couldn't see if she was in the car.

Moving quickly but soundlessly, he came around the red truck and checked the driver's seat. Empty. He wasn't about to stop and take notes, but a quick glance at the front of the car confirmed this person was driving on New York plates.

Logan scooted down the steep grass-covered ditch beside the road, balancing himself with his free hand. Something moved at the side of Addison's car. A man was trying to open the driver's side door.

He had two choices. Go in quietly and hope to sneak up on the guy, risking that the creep might get to Addison first. Or scare the shit out of him now and make sure he kept his grubby hands to himself. Logan couldn't see Addison, but it appeared as though she'd locked the door per his instruction.

Good girl, Addi. I'm coming for you, just hang in there.

All of a sudden a loud snapping sound cut through the night. *Shit!* A branch crunched beneath his feet and the guy froze next to Addison's door.

"Back away from the car," Logan said calmly, the gun pointed straight forward. His voice carried across the clearing.

"I was just trying to help her, man." The guy popped his hands up by his head and took a step back.

His face was covered by a hood, and despite the balmy weather, he had on long sleeves, gloves and jeans.

"You normally wear gloves in the summer?" Logan advanced, moving quicker now that he didn't need to keep quiet.

The other man continued walking backward, heading toward the edge of the trees. He was going to run; Logan could feel it in his bones. But he still couldn't tell if Addison was okay, and time wouldn't allow him to have it both ways. He could check on her *or* he could go after the guy. Blindly shooting at a man wasn't an option, even if Logan was positive that this guy was aiming to do *anything* but help her.

"Hold up," he called out. "That's far enough."

The guy slowed down for a second, but his twitchy movements told Logan he wouldn't stay put long. The car was close, but the damn darkness hid what was inside. If Addison was hurt, he needed to get to her. Now.

Then the guy turned and took off like a shot. Logan swore under his breath and broke into a sprint. Tall grass whipped past his legs, his shoes catching over a dip in the ground and tripping him up. Blood rushed in his ears, his heart pounding with adrenaline. All he could see was the back of the guy's hoodie as he disappeared into the trees.

Logan skidded to a stop at the side of the Audi, his gun still pointing ahead. But the area was dark and he'd have no hope of catching the guy now. Leaning down to the passenger side window, he found Addison inside. Her tearstained face looked up at him, relief seeping into her features.

He'd found her. And now he wouldn't be letting her out of his sight.

3

ADDISON'S HANDS TREMBLED so much that she struggled to open the door. The whole crazy event had happened in a blur. After the truck rammed her, the Audi had skidded off the road and hurtled down a small hill. Luckily, her brakes were in fine working order and she'd avoided crashing into the trees.

But being trapped in the car while some crazy person tried to wrench the door open was easily the most terrifying thing she'd ever experienced. He'd been hunting around for something to break the glass when Logan had showed up.

What if that lunatic had been able to get inside? How would you have defended yourself then?

The warm summer air filtered into the car as Addison finally got the door open. Then Logan's hands were on her, helping her stand. He wrapped his arms around her so she could stay upright on her shaking legs. She melted against him, needing something solid and real to keep her from falling into a heap.

"Are you okay?" His hand brushed the hair from her forehead—but the gesture wasn't tender. He was checking for injuries. His thumb snagged a sore spot and she winced.

"I don't think anything is broken," she said. "But I bumped my head."

He checked her over as best he could in the dark. Her cheek throbbed and she was pretty sure there would be bruising on her chest from the seat belt. But she was in one piece, which was a whole lot better than what would have happened if her attacker had gotten inside her car.

"I should take you to the hospital," Logan said, continuing to inspect her.

"No, I'm okay."

"Are you sure? I'll have to keep an eye on you in case there are signs of concussion." He scanned her face. "If anything feels off, you have to tell me, okay?"

"Okay." Her eyes darted to the dark patch of forest in front of her.

"He's gone, Addi."

That's when she noticed the gun in his hand. "You didn't shoot him?"

"I'm not going to open fire on the side of the road." He looked down at her, less analytical this time. His rich brown eyes searched her face. "Not unless I need to. You know the rule."

"Guns are the last resort," she repeated her father's words and pressed her hand to her head. Squeezing her eyes shut against the throbbing, her heart rate slowed. "But the bastard got away."

"I wasn't going to risk leaving you by yourself in the car in case you were hurt." He pulled her to his chest and rested his chin on top of her head. "You come first, remember?"

Her stomach pitched. This was how he'd held her before all her boundaries turned to shit two years ago. That simple movement of tucking her head against the crook of his neck, cradling her like she was the most precious thing in the whole world, had obliterated her. Her hand came to his chest, her fingers curling into his soft cotton T-shirt.

For a moment they stood there, silent and unmoving. His hand cupped the back of her head, his warmth seeping into her. The furious beating of his heart vibrated under her fingertips. From the outside no one would know that he was worried—he hadn't broken a sweat, hadn't lost his cool. But she could feel his fear. His care.

"What the hell do we do now?" she asked, pushing away from him and bracing her hand against the damaged car. She couldn't deal with Logan being kind to her, not knowing that soon she'd be leaving him. Distance was important right now. "I hit something pretty hard on the way down. I have no idea if I can drive this thing."

Logan crouched and checked under the car. "It's possible you've bent the axle. Let's leave it here and I'll call a tow truck when we get to the cottage."

They grabbed her things and walked up to where Logan's car sat on the side of the road. The red truck was still there, so he took a photo of the plate and tried the doors. Locked. Nothing helpful could be seen through the windows.

An hour later they were settled at the cottage. Logan had called a tow company for Addison's car and had reported the incident to the police. Tomorrow they'd head to the local station and make a statement in person. But chances were, whoever had chased Addison off the road would go back to collect his vehicle. Logan couldn't leave Addison alone at the cottage, however. And potentially putting her in harm's way by taking her back to the scene wasn't an option, either. So the pictures of the vehicle would have to do.

"He'll probably clean it out and then dump it somewhere," Logan said as they sat at the dining table eating her lasagna. He was in full-on work mode now. "It'll turn up, but if he's smart there won't be much for the police to go on."

"You really think it's the guy who wrote me the email?" She poured them both another glass of wine, concentrating so that her hand didn't shake.

"It would be a hell of a coincidence if it wasn't. I mean, road rage happens, but if you say you didn't do anything to antagonize the guy—"

"I didn't."

"Then why would some stranger run you off the road for no reason?" He shook his head, his brow furrowed. "No, it has to be him."

"But how would he know that I was coming out to the cottage? That I'd be on that road?"

"How would he know your email address? He might be following you. He might have hacked into your laptop. It could be a number of things." Logan forked a piece of lasagna into his mouth. "In any case, we'll figure it out. No need to worry, we're in this together."

"I'm not worried," she lied.

Maybe it was stupid, but she didn't want Logan to suspect how much the incident had shaken her. Sometimes she wished she'd gone into the security side of the business like she'd wanted to—then she'd be better prepared for these kinds of incidents. Instead, she'd studied business because she had a natural talent for numbers and her father had said that's what the company needed from her. What *he* needed from her. And she never could say no to him.

Still, she wondered if he'd only said that as another way of trying to protect her. In reality, all it had done was leave her without the respect of her staff.

She shoved the thoughts aside. The last thing she needed was to crumble now and prove to Logan that she couldn't handle this situation.

"You have every right to be worried, Addi." He looked up from his meal. "Most people would be in pieces after what you went through tonight."

"I'm *not* most people. I've heard all of Dad's stories and all of yours. I can deal with this."

His eyes softened and a ghost of a smile passed over his full lips. "I am well aware of that."

"I don't want you to think that you need to be my bodyguard or anything." She pushed her food around on her plate for a moment before abandoning it and reaching for her wine. "I'll be okay."

He looked like he was about to argue, but instead he rubbed the back of his neck. Whenever Logan was trying to figure something out, he kneaded that particular spot. It was the tell that'd allowed her to kick his butt in poker for years. For some reason, it made her belly flip watching his strong hands work at the muscle like that.

Her mind wouldn't let her forget how it felt to have those hands on her. Caressing her. Holding her. Dragging her into position. He was the perfect blend of rough and smooth—hard and soft—and he walked the line between them with delicious ease.

"I made a promise and I intend to keep it." He leaned back in his chair, his eyes smoothing over her. Filling her with liquid heat.

"What if I don't want you hanging around and being my shadow?" Or worse, what if she *did* want it?

"Worried it might upset the guys you date?" He raised a brow. "I can be discreet."

It would have pleased her to no end to tell him that guys were lining up at her door, but the truth was far lonelier than that. Most of the men she met were terrified of Logan—he was like an overprotective big brother. Except he happened to be a crack shot and had a military background to boot.

When she started dating someone, he'd make a point to "drop in" and introduce himself to the guy. Not once had he outright told someone to stay away from her, but then again her dates didn't usually stick around long enough for her to find out if Logan would take that next step.

"I'll believe that when I see it," she said drily.

"What? You won't even know I'm there."

"Are you going to sit in the corner and watch while I take a guy to bed?" It was clear from the way his jaw twitched that her words had made their mark. "What? You moved on after we slept together, so why shouldn't I?"

"I told you I regretted what happened." His voice was tight. Brittle.

"It's too late for regrets." She carved off a small piece of lasagna and forked it into her mouth. It tasted of nothing. "And you're not my father, Logan. You don't get to vet my dates."

"I know that."

"And you can't keep watch over me twenty-four/seven."

He folded his arms over his chest, the muscles curving outward. Defined and honed to perfection. "I will be until we figure out who's after you."

He wore a fitted black T-shirt—his uniform—and damn, it looked so good her mouth watered. Ugh, why couldn't she be attracted to normal men who didn't have hero complexes?

But as much as she was loath to admit it, he made her feel safer than anyone else on the face of the earth.

"You can't have it both ways."

"What's that supposed to mean?" His eyes flashed. "I'm trying to do the right thing."

"By chasing off any chance I have of finding a decent man? Anyone who gets close to me is treated like a potential terrorist. Then they quickly decide I'm not worth the trouble."

Frustration bubbled up within her; the argument was well-worn between them. Normally she was able to tell Logan to go to hell and get on with her day. But not now, not after he'd been proven right. Not after she'd almost been…

The reality of her situation suddenly crashed over her like a wave. Someone had run her off the road; they'd tried to get her out of her car. She'd been trapped like an animal in a cage of her own making, defenseless. Vulnerable.

If he hadn't shown up, God only knew what might have happened to her.

"You *are* worth the trouble, Addi." He raked a hand through his longish hair. "Fuck, I'm sorry that I'm such a thorn in your side. But I can't *not* take care of you…"

For a moment she studied him. It was easy to see why women went crazy over Logan—the overlong, light brown hair, heavy brows and strong jaw made him look dangerous. Powerful. His hands were rough and calloused; his muscles were rock solid. There wasn't anything polished about him. Not even running a successful company for two years had smoothed his sharp edges.

There was a rawness to him, a brutal honesty, and an unfiltered, unbridled passion for what he believed in.

"I guess I could assign one of my guys to look out for you. One of them might be a little less..." A crease formed between his brows. "Intense."

"You wouldn't trust someone else to do what you think is your job," she said, shaking her head. "That's the problem. You're trying to take responsibility for me when I'm telling you that I'm a grown woman. I want to live my life."

"But you never know what kind of shit people are hiding. All I'm saying is that you need to do some due diligence, especially now." He paused. "You're too trusting."

She gulped the remainder of her wine, feeling a slight sense of relief as the alcohol wore down her nervous energy. "You've got to be kidding me. After the way you treated me, I don't trust *anyone*."

He stood suddenly, pushing the dining chair back so hard it almost toppled over. "I said I was sorry, Addison. Christ, what more can I do? I crossed a line, I realized my mistake, and I made a promise that it would never happen again."

And by "crossed a line" of course he meant that he'd given her the greatest night in her very sheltered existence. The moment Logan had walked into her father's office as a damaged, angry twenty-two-year-old, she'd been in love. Her sixteen-year-old self had fallen hard and fast.

But Logan had been Mr. Morals when it came to her—except for that one night. But then he'd moved on so quickly that she'd gotten whiplash from it.

"We had sex, Logan. You make it sound like you forced me." She pushed her food away, her stomach twisting itself into knots. "I *wanted* it. God, how I wanted it—"

"Stop." He held up a hand like she was some misbehaving toddler and instantly regretted it.

But hearing her talk about how she'd wanted him was more than he could take. It was more than his resolve could take. Walking out of Addison's apartment the morning after they'd been together had been the hardest thing he'd ever done. Ignoring her hurt had damn near killed him. But it had been the right thing to do. Because he'd promised her father he would care for her.

Not fuck her.

Fire flashed in her dark eyes. "Am I that hideous that you can't even stand being reminded of what we did?"

Hideous? "You're out of your mind if you think I wasn't right there with you."

"Then why did you run out of there like a bat out of hell the next morning?" Her hands twisted in her lap.

The red lacquer on her nails glinted in the light. It was the only remaining sign of the hyperpolished image she presented at the office. She must have changed for the drive—gone were the sexy heels and stockings, gone were the pearl earrings and the tight skirt. Instead, she wore a pair of soft jeans that hugged her small hips and long legs. A loose white T-shirt revealed a hint of a pink bra beneath.

Addison had a thing for lingerie, and now so did he.

Before her, he'd been happy to have a girl as she'd been made—without a stitch of clothing. But Addison had taught him to appreciate lace and silk and those damn fiddly clasps that held her stockings up. All in one night, she'd changed him. Changed what he liked, what he craved.

What he wanted for his future.

"It was a mistake," he said, swallowing hard against the lump in his throat.

It was the best mistake he'd ever made.

"Why?" she demanded. "We were two consenting adults. We used protection and we didn't do it in public. Our having sex hardly threw the world off its axis."

Except it did—his world, anyway. "You're like family to me—"

"Oh, spare me." She pushed up from her chair. "We're not related, thank God."

What the hell was he supposed to say? That he walked away because he was terrified of screwing things up? Or that something might happen to her and that he'd flip out and lose his grip on reality? Again.

Or that when he was with her he couldn't seem to control himself and that scared the hell out of him?

"The reason I walked away had *nothing* to do with my attraction to you." He rolled his shoulders back and tried to dispel the tension in his limbs. "That wasn't a factor."

"So you *were* attracted to me?"

He cleared his throat. "Of course I was."

"It wasn't a pity fuck? You know, because of…" She blinked and straightened her shoulders. "Because Dad had just died."

He gritted his teeth and tried to keep his voice at an appropriate volume. "No."

"Are you still attracted to me?" She stepped forward.

It was too much: her messy blond hair, the wine on her lips. The hungry look in her eyes.

"I'm not answering that."

She stepped closer again and now he could smell the faint remains of perfume on her skin. Chanel No. 5. He'd bought her a bottle for her birthday. Damn expensive crap that smelled like old ladies in the bottle but transformed into heaven on her skin.

"Why not?"

"Because that's not why I'm here."

"Right, I forgot. You're playing bodyguard." She rolled her eyes. "You know I always did have a thing for role-playing."

Tension snapped in the air between them and she seemed about to say more, but she simply shook her head and turned back to the table. Plates clattered as she cleared up their abandoned meal.

"One day you'll push me away hard enough that I won't come back," she said quietly.

"What's that supposed to mean?" His stomach knotted as a sense of foreboding fell over him.

"I'm just saying that it won't always be like this. Change happens and I might not always be around."

Change. A dirty fucking word as far as he was concerned. Change always meant pain; it always meant loss. And loss meant destruction.

"I don't want things to change."

"We don't always get what we want, now do we?" she said, not looking at him. "Anyway, you'll need to make up the bed in one of the spare rooms. I was going to do that over the weekend. You remember where the sheets are?"

"Yeah."

"I'll see you in the morning."

He'd been dismissed, apparently. By trying to do the right thing, he'd screwed up again. It seemed to be his lot in life.

"Probably for the best," he muttered to himself.

He wasn't cut out to care about people, because loss was inevitable and it turned him into a wild beast. Losing his mother had ended his military career, losing Daniel had sent him straight into Addison's arms, and if he lost her…who the hell knew what he'd do.

But that didn't mean he didn't want her. Far from it. He just knew that he couldn't act on his desires.

4

LOGAN SET HIMSELF up on the couch with his laptop and a cup of decaf. He was far too wired to sleep, and his vantage point allowed him to watch the thin beam of light from under Addison's bedroom door. Every so often a shadow flickered, telling him she was unpacking and setting up her room.

Being run off the road wasn't enough to deter her from organizing every little thing the way she liked it.

He smiled to himself. She'd always been that way—needing to have everything just so. Teenage Addison had been a straight-A student with neat-freak tendencies. She used to visit her dad at the office after school and would happily spend hours reorganizing his filing system and making sure the staff kitchen was clean and tidy. Logan had always pretended not to notice her, of course.

Daniel had once told him that Addison developed her organizational habits after her mother died. A sense of order in her physical environment had helped her sift through the pain and confusion in her head, apparently. Her father had encouraged her to take those skills and turn them into a fruitful career, which she had. Addison was the reason Cobalt & Dane had been able to grow as a company. Without her, they'd still be a couple of scruffy guys too focused on the security side of things to get the rent paid.

He envied her ability to turn her loss into something useful. His pain never seemed to cause anything but pure destruction.

Sighing, he raked a hand through his hair and stared at the laptop screen. Going through his emails might help him relax. Daniel had set up an extensive security system when he'd first bought the cottage, so the chance of anything happening without Logan's knowledge was slim.

Eventually the light under Addison's door disappeared, but that didn't stop Logan's gaze from wandering there every few minutes. This weekend would be torture. Bittersweet torture.

"Lucky you're a natural-born masochist," Logan muttered to himself.

After an hour of trying—and failing—to get any work done, he snapped his laptop shut in frustration. If he wasn't going to be productive then he'd go to bed and attempt to sleep. A few hours of shut-eye might help his concentration.

"Yeah, 'cause sleep is the problem," he grumbled as he walked past Addison's door to the linen cupboard.

It was packed with clean sheets, towels and blankets and smelled musty in a way that brought a rush of memories to him. He'd come to this cottage often, spending Thanksgiving weekend with Daniel and Addison since his own father had made it clear he wasn't welcome with the shiny new family he'd acquired. Those long weekends had been filled with fishing, eating and letting Addison beat him at poker until she got good enough that she whipped his ass all on her own.

His fingertips brushed a piece of floral fabric sandwiched between two plain blue sheets. The flowers had faces, but the pattern had faded over the years. Time, the cruel mistress that it was, had robbed them of their smiles.

A noise caused Logan to turn. He tiptoed to Addison's door and pressed his ear to the wood. The muffled sobbing caused pain to wrench in his chest. He touched his palm to the door and sucked in a breath. What the hell was he supposed to do in this situation?

If Addison was in danger, he wouldn't hesitate to act, because protecting her came second nature to him. But a tearful Addison was totally outside his experience. The only other time he'd seen her cry was at her father's funeral…and look how that'd turned out.

He should walk away. Let her cry it out and emerge in the morning with her mask intact. Isn't that what she'd want?

Walk away, you useless son of a bitch. Be a deserter. Isn't that what you do best?

Logan gritted his teeth and eased the handle down on her bedroom door. The room was dark, with only a thin shaft of moonlight illuminating the bed. The cool bluish light showed the outline of her sleeping form. The curve of her hip and the gentle dip at her waist. The soft gleam of her blond hair.

"Addi?" He let the door shut behind him.

She was crying, more softly now. As his eyes adjusted to the dark, he could make out the tremble in her curled-up form. She was facing away from him, her body so small and vulnerable in the center of the large bed.

"Addi? Are you okay?"

She muttered something under her breath and then sighed, but he couldn't make out the words. For years he'd teased her about the way she talked in her sleep— he'd witnessed it on the few occasions when she'd fallen asleep on his couch after having an argument with her dad. Sometimes it was a soft jumble of syllables and other times it was full sentences. Often the words had no meaning.

"Logan," she sighed.

He tiptoed over to her bed and knelt on the mattress with one knee. Both her eyes were shut and her cheeks were damp with tears. The wet skin seemed to shimmer in the bright moonlight. But she slept on.

And dreamed about him, apparently.

He brushed his knuckles along her arm, his breath sticking in his throat when she shivered at his touch. Her body was covered by a white sheet, but a spaghetti-thin strap of black silk curved over her shoulder and a hint of lace peeked out from the top of the sheet.

Sweet mother of—

"Logan?" She shifted on the bed, her voice groggy.

"It's just me, Addi. I heard you crying." He brushed the hair away from her face.

"I was sleeping."

"I didn't mean to wake you. I came in to check that you were okay." His heart thudded in his chest so hard it felt like the organ was trying to punch its way out of his rib cage.

"Oh?" She touched her fingers to her cheek. "I must have been dreaming."

"I'll let you sleep." He pulled away, but she rolled and reached out for him. The movement caused the sheet to slip farther down, revealing a black silk camisole gleaming under the moonlight. The glossy fabric looked almost wet.

"Stay for a minute," she said sleepily.

Maybe *he* was the one dreaming. Addison never asked him to stay with her for anything, not these days. The car accident must have shaken her worse than she'd let on.

"Lie with me. Just until I fall back to sleep." She tugged him to her and he lowered himself onto the bed. "I had trouble drifting off before."

Propping himself up on one elbow, he rubbed his hand up and down her arm. Her skin was clammy. Damp.

"Hmm." She mumbled under her breath and turned so she was facing the wall again. "That's nice."

He tried to pull the sheet back up, but she swatted him away with a protest about being hot. Little did she know it was more for him than it was for her. The sight of her bare skin against the black silk was jacking up his pulse. Not to mention he was fighting off the beginnings of a rock-hard erection.

All you have to do is get her to drift off, then you can back away. Tomorrow, you'll pretend you never came in here.

He kept a few inches between them as he lay down beside her, but she wriggled until her back lined his chest, the curve of her ass cradled perfectly in his lap. A jolt of arousal shot through him, but he held his breath and forced down the excitement. It was like trying to swallow a pill without water.

"What if you hadn't followed me tonight?" she whispered groggily. "What would have happened if…if…"

A tremor ran through her body and he wrapped his

arm around her, hugging her to his chest. "I'll find this guy and take him down, I swear."

"I want to take care of myself."

He held his tongue. There was no point arguing with her now—he knew how she felt about being independent. About wanting to prove that she could handle things on her own. Of course, he disagreed. She wasn't weak, far from it. In fact, Addison was the strongest person he knew. But she didn't have his training, his experience.

Daniel had sheltered her from the ugly aspects of their world, and to the best of his ability, Logan would continue that. He could never lose her, never let anything happen to her. Because without her...well, he didn't even want to think about a world where she wasn't part of his life.

"I want to take care of you, for once." Her whispered voice prickled at his resolve; it picked apart his defenses.

His brain scrambled to find the right thing to say, but that had never been his forte. Some guys had a knack for words; they knew how to seduce and influence and placate. But Logan was only good with his hands.

"Shhh." He brushed her hair back, smoothing his fingertips over her temple with each stroke. "You need to sleep now."

For a moment he thought she'd drifted off; her breathing became soft and her body seemed to melt against his. He'd been holding himself in check but the slight shift of her body, the gentlest brush of her ass against his lap, yanked open the floodgates. His cock leaped from half-mast to full attention and a groan stuck in his throat.

As he was about to extricate himself from her bed, she moved again. This time he realized it was on purpose, and knowing that made him even harder. His brain screamed at him to go, but she felt so damn good in his arms. Soft yet firm, silky smooth. So tempting.

"Logan," she breathed, rolling her head back against his chest. Her hand slipped between them and she felt for his cock. His whole body was about to go up in flames.

Yeah, flames. Because you're going straight to hell.

"Addi, we shouldn't—"

"Shh." Her fingers danced along the length of his fly. He strained painfully against the confines of his jeans, the zipper barely keeping him in. "I can feel how much you want it."

"It's not about my wants," he gritted out. How could he be so weak to end up in this position again?

"Is it about what *I* want?" Her hand moved away from his cock and he thought he might be off the hook. But she captured his wrist and pulled his hand down until he cupped her between the legs.

Heat radiated through the sheet. Even with the material stopping him from fully exploring her, he could feel how ready she was. She kept her hand over his as she circled her hips into his touch.

"Dammit, Addi." He moaned into her hair. It was all he could do not to rip the sheet from her body and plunge his fingers into her sweet, hot sex. "This isn't right. Last time was…"

"Sex, Logan. It was sex." She huffed. "I'm not some delicate flower, you know."

She pushed the sheet down, exposing the full glory of the silk camisole as it hugged her incredible body. When she pushed up to straddle him, her breasts bounced, unconfined. He remembered how she'd felt under his tongue, the way her rosy little nipples had stiffened when he'd kissed them. The way her back had bowed when he'd sucked on them. The way her skin had tasted sweet and earthy and unique.

"I can read you like a book." She pressed down, tilting her hips back and forth so that she rubbed her sex along the hard length of him. The sensation was too good; he forced his eyes shut and his fingers dug into her hips. "You want me."

If he wasn't careful that gentle rocking of her hips was going to make him come in his pants. But he couldn't seem to push her away. She was right—he wanted her. He wanted her more than the air in his lungs.

Always had, always would…against his better judgment, anyway.

"If you don't stop that, I'm not going to be able to walk away."

A wicked smile curved on her full lips. "I doubt you'd be able to walk anywhere right now."

ADDISON SWIRLED HER hips in a figure eight, feeling the rasp of Logan's jeans against her sensitive skin. Hovering over him—knowing he was fully at her mercy—was a power trip. In every other aspect of their lives he was in charge; he was one step ahead.

She might not be able to have control in the boardroom, but in the bedroom…this could be her domain. *This* was where she could gain control back, where she could have the upper hand.

You sure it's nothing to do with the fact that you could have died tonight? That you could have lost him for good?

Fear wrapped its hands around her throat but she shoved the troubling thoughts away. Now was not the time for weakness. She leaned forward, hinging at her hips and giving him an eyeful of her breasts. Obviously she hadn't packed the camisole for him, since she was supposed to be spending the weekend alone. She simply loved the feel of silk on her skin.

But she liked the feel of his hands on her even more.

"Keep pushing me, Addi. I dare you." His face was hard-set, the angle of his jaw sharp in the near darkness.

"I'm not afraid of you," she whispered, bending forward so that her lips brushed his ear. "Everyone thinks you're the Big Bad Wolf but I know you're just a teddy bear."

His big hands slid along her thighs, catching the hem of the camisole and pushing it up. "Is that so?"

"Mmm-hmm."

His hands inched higher. "You're making one terrible mistake right now."

"What's that?"

His thumb brushed the sensitive skin of her sex. "Thinking you're in charge just because you're on top."

Before she could retort, he felt for her clit with his thumb. Pleasure rocketed through her the second he made contact and she fell back, bracing herself on her hands. It was shameless how she thrust her hips toward him, determined to get as much friction as possible. The slow, sensual seduction was over.

That exactly was what Logan was like in bed. To the point. He didn't mess around. Rather, he went straight in for the kill.

"Oh God." Her head lolled. "You're too damn good at that."

"Tell me how good," he urged her on, his voice shredded and rough. "If I'm going to hell I want to know you've enjoyed the ride."

A low chuckle came from her throat. "And you still say you're in charge?"

He grunted and grabbed her hips, yanking her forward and pushing himself down on the mattress at the same time until her body hovered over his face. Was he going to…?

He latched his mouth onto her sex and his tongue lapped at her with a focus that made her whole body quake. Tremors racked her, but his hands held her down over him. She pitched forward and planted one hand on the wall behind the bed to stop herself from falling over.

"Logan!" His name dissolved on her tongue as orgasm swept through her. Her muscles clenched and released as pleasure poured through her veins. Obliterating her. Turning her to mush.

As the tremors subsided, he guided her back down to the bed. She curled into him, her hands seeking out the warmth of his chest and the vibrations of his heart.

"Score one, Team Dane," he said as he wrapped his arms around her.

"Screw you."

He chuckled against her hair. "Is that a request?"

"It's an order."

The ridge outlined by his jeans told her that he was at bursting point. That meant she'd have to take it slow, tease him for as long as she could before giving in. Prove to him that he wasn't in charge here. This was *her* domain.

She drew his zipper down, the sound cutting through the quiet. Thankfully he hadn't worn a belt today, so all she had to do was pop the button at his waist. His cock strained forward, peeking out the top of his boxer briefs.

"Who's in charge now?" She drew him out slowly,

reveling in the way he tried to conceal his moan by clamping his teeth together. The twitch in his jaw gave him away entirely.

"You know I am, Addison."

"I don't think so." Wrapping her fingers around him, she moved her fist up and down his length, giving his tip a light squeeze with every stroke. "You're at my mercy now."

His hips bucked as she increased her pace. A string of curse words flew out of his lips as she bent forward and ran her tongue over the swollen head of him. The taste of him flooded her with memories. That night... that sweaty, passionate, dirty night.

"Say it," she said, blowing cool air over his heated skin.

"No." He ground the word out, but he was already fishing around in his pants. He found his wallet and flipped it open.

"I won't let you finish until you do." Her strokes slowed and she watched him, her whole body alight with energy.

"You started this," he said, pulling out a foil packet and tearing it open. "I'm going to finish it...and then I'm going to finish you again."

Pushing her hands out of the way, he rolled the condom down his length. That simple action had never excited her with other men—it was the business part of sex. No glove, no love, right? But watching Logan handle himself intoxicated her. Arousal hung over her like a heavy cloud; it fogged her mind, and she didn't protest when he reached for her hips again, dragging her into place and seating himself deep inside her.

Being filled by him was a pleasure of the most exquisite variety. He fit perfectly inside her, as if he'd been designed for her.

"No arguments?" he asked with a sly smile.

"I'm still on top." She planted her hands on his chest as he thrust up into her.

"We can fix that."

In a second, he'd flipped her onto her back and had pinned her hands above her head. His hot breath whispered over her skin as he kissed her neck, sucking and biting until she writhed beneath him.

Damn him. He knew exactly what to do.

"Don't fight it, baby. I'm better when I'm in charge."

When his mouth came down on her hers, she was lost. The insistent press of his tongue, the stubble on his jaw and the faint taste of herself on his lips was enough to send her over the edge again. She pressed her face against his neck and chanted his name over and over as her body shook.

"That's it, tell me." He pumped into her faster. "Tell me."

"It's you, Logan. It's you."

He thrust into her once more and roared as he found his release. Cradling her in his arms, he rolled them onto their sides and threw one thigh over her. Claiming her.

Reminding her that tomorrow she'd need to regain her distance if she had any hope of protecting her heart....

5

ADDISON'S EYES SNAPPED open at the sound of a bird chirping outside her window. The blare of horns and wail of sirens that usually greeted her in the morning were suspiciously absent. She pushed herself up and blew the hair out of her eyes to see that she wasn't in her sleek and stylish Manhattan apartment.

Of course, she was at the cottage.

The events of last night came rushing over her like an avalanche. The long drive, the car accident, fighting with Logan…making up with Logan.

"Ugh." She ground the heels of her palms into her eyes.

There would be no escaping Logan this weekend, not if she might be in danger. A delicious shiver rippled through Addison's body. Everything ached in that way that could be achieved only by orgasms and hot, spontaneous sex. It had been too long since she'd felt this good, *far* too long.

The empty space in the bed was cool and fairly unrumpled, which meant he hadn't stayed long. Not that she was surprised. When it came to the morning-after dash, Logan made Usain Bolt look slow.

A dark thought tugged at the corner of her mind. Last time she *had* been taken by surprise, because she'd been stupid enough to think that he might want to stick around. That he might feel something real for her. But less than a week later, she'd turned up at his apartment to find another woman answering his front door.

That's not going to happen this time. You know the score, and you've got plans to make it on your own. Sex doesn't change that.

And having sex with Logan was fine so long as it suited her needs: pleasure for her body, but not for her heart. She didn't regret seducing him last night, not even a little bit. Being in his arms—distracting herself from the night's events—was exactly what she'd needed. But that was *all* she needed from him.

Addison threw on her bathing suit and then layered a floaty cotton dress over the top. This weekend was going to be all about rest and relaxation, regardless of whether or not Logan wanted to participate. No one was going to get her down—not him, not the guy who'd run her off the road. No one.

LOGAN PACED THE length of the deck out on the back of the cottage. The morning sun was light and buttery yellow. Soft, beautiful. Like Addison.

Christ, you're comparing her to the morning sun now? Get a fucking grip.

He raked a hand through his hair and stared across the land that stretched out in front of him. It was so peaceful here, so serene. But all he could feel was how isolated they were. How no one would hear or see them.

They could do anything and the world would be none the wiser.

Having that level of freedom wasn't a good thing for a man like Logan. He needed to know someone was watching, keeping tabs. In the office, he had guys like Rhys and Owen and Aiden to keep him in check. *His* team, his men. They didn't realize it, but they kept him in line. Simply by giving him their loyalty, he was bound to do right by them as Daniel had done for him. But out here, anything was possible.

And that scared the shit out of him.

"Morning," Addison said as she came up next to him. Her hair flowed loosely around her shoulders, her legs and feet bare under her summer dress.

He wasn't sure how he should greet her. With a kiss, or would that be too familiar? A hug, perhaps. But that could be too brotherly.

This is exactly why you shouldn't have overstepped. You got all caught up in the passion of the moment and then things got weird.

He had too much to lose by getting entangled with Addison—it wasn't just that he'd be dishonoring the memory of the man who'd mentored him. The company was his whole life, and he needed Addison by his side to take care of all the things he was clueless about: finances, health and safety, and all that other administrative crap that made his eyes turn square. Sure, there were other people who could do her job, but none who would do it as well as her. None that he trusted.

She was Cobalt and he was Dane. Without one of those elements, Cobalt & Dane didn't exist. Which meant he couldn't risk any type of personal relationship with her. Especially given his track record for screwing things up.

"Fancy a coffee?" she asked, eyeing him with unconcealed curiosity. "I've just put the pot on."

"You're speaking my language."

He followed her back into the house and closed the door behind him, flicking the lock. A good security system wasn't worth crap if you didn't make use of it.

Addison swanned around the kitchen, humming to herself. She didn't seem adversely affected by last night…though he wasn't sure what he'd been expecting. They hadn't made any rules or set any boundaries.

"So, uh…about last night," he said, sliding onto a stool at the edge of the kitchen's island counter.

"Yeah?" Addison raised a brow as she placed two mugs next to the coffeepot.

"Should we…talk?" He drummed his fingers on the countertop. "Or something?"

"I'd like to know what the 'or something' is before I say yes," she teased. Steam curled up from the mugs as she poured their drinks.

"You get what I mean."

"It's just sex, Logan. It was consensual. We used protection." She shrugged. "What more should we discuss?"

"I don't know. I just figured that's what women normally like to do afterward."

She laughed. "The women you date might like to talk afterward, but I'm fine."

Truth be told, he'd never tried to initiate a conversation after sex before, so he had *no* idea what women wanted.

"I don't expect anything from you," she said, placing his coffee in front of him. "If that's what you're worried about. It wasn't anything more than blowing off steam."

"Right."

"I'm not going to ask you for any commitment. Whether we do it again or not…" She shrugged. "It's no-strings in my mind."

He wasn't sure how he felt about her assessment—was it possible to be both relieved and disappointed at the same time? Her silky skin was still freshly imprinted on his memory. His palms tingled with the urge to touch her again, but they had business to take care of. And forty-eight more hours until the rest of their team showed up.

"We should head down to the police station and make our report today," he said, blowing at the curl of steam winding up from his coffee. "What do you remember about the guy?"

Her eyes dropped, long pale lashes obscuring her rich brown eyes for a moment. "Not much. It was dark and it all happened so quickly."

"What was he wearing?"

Logan remembered, of course. He'd cataloged that information away the second he'd spotted the guy. But starting with a simpler and more obvious detail was a technique often used to unlock memories. Memories could be followed like bread crumbs until something useful was found.

"His face was hard to see—he had a hood covering it." She sucked on her lower lip, her eyes fixated on something in the distance. "He had gloves on, too."

"Did you see his face at all? Were there any marks or tattoos?"

She shook her head. "He was white, but beyond that…"

"Did he say anything to you?"

Addison raised the mug to her lips, her hand trembling. "He said 'let me in, you fucking bitch' but I don't know what that's going to tell us."

"He didn't ask you anything? Did he call you by name?"

"No. So I'm not sure what the police will be able to do." The doubt in her tone belied the neutral expression on her face. He suspected she didn't want to seem scared, but after last night they were well beyond pretending how she felt.

Still, he knew Addison. She had to feel in control at all times. This situation must be eating her up inside because it was something she couldn't dictate.

"They'll chase down the vehicle and ask around some of the local businesses to see if anyone spotted him. That kind of thing. It might not yield any leads, but we have to try."

She nodded. "Okay."

"You didn't notice anything suspicious when you stopped at the gas station, did you? Was anyone following you?"

"No, I don't think so." She scrunched up her nose as she tried to remember. "Actually, there was this one guy who leered at me, but I don't know if you'd call that suspicious."

Men staring at Addison was hardly something he'd find unusual, either, but he'd come to realize in his line of work that even the smallest piece of information was worth looking at. "Did he say anything to you?"

"No, at least not that I heard. I was on the phone to you so I turned away."

"What kind of a car was he driving?"

"A truck." Her brow creased suddenly. "It might have been a red truck. I can't quite remember but…"

"But?"

"I think it was red." Her skin had become pale, wan. Her coffee sat untouched on the island countertop. "Maybe he was watching me for longer than I realized."

"But you didn't notice anyone following you on the road."

"It's a straight road, Logan. Everyone's going in the same direction and I didn't notice anything until he got too close."

"It's okay, Addi. We'll tell the police about the guy at the gas station and they should be able to get a hold of the security cameras. Then we'll know if it was the same person."

She nodded, but her eyes didn't meet his.

A few hours later—after they'd been to the local police station and reported the incident to Addison's insurance company—Logan logged into his work email. Since it was the weekend, nothing much had come through, but Rhys had checked in to confirm that he was still welcome at the retreat. Logan chuckled to himself. His IT manager was a rule-follower to a tee.

"I think you owe Rhys an apology," he said, glancing up from his screen.

Addison sat on the couch with her long legs stretched out, the edge of her sundress tantalizingly brushing the tops of her thighs. "We're incentivizing staff disobedience now, are we? I thought you of all people would understand the consequences of not following orders no matter how someone personally feels about the situation."

"That's a low blow."

Her defenses had to be up if she was using his past to make her point. Not that he could blame her entirely;

she'd had a rough day. The officer at the local station hadn't seemed too interested in her report—then he'd asked a few pointed questions about her driving history, which had gotten Addison's back up. Luckily, Logan had been able to stop her from storming out of the station. Still, he wasn't holding his breath for anything useful to come from the report.

"I'm just saying that Rhys wouldn't have gone against something *you* told him to do." She tucked a strand of blond hair behind her ears. "I would simply like the same level of respect."

"The staff *do* respect you. But I train them to follow their instincts. Security staff are useless if they ignore what their guts tell them. Luckily, I didn't fire him as you asked," he joked, but she flashed him an irritated look. "He was worried about you, that's all. It wasn't meant to be a sign of disrespect."

Her red nails clicked on the keys of her laptop as she typed. He'd grown to enjoy the sound as he often heard it coming from her office late in the evenings when they were the only two people left.

"What are you working on?"

"Just preparations for Monday. You know, what I'd planned to do before you gate-crashed my weekend." She didn't turn away from her screen, but the corner of her lip twitched.

"Glad to hear I'm always welcome."

THE NEXT FEW days dragged for Logan, which wasn't unusual. The retreat always made him restless because he hated to be away from the action. His hands would twitch with the need to do something, while all of

Addison's reports and numbers made his head spin. And made his mind go numb.

But this time his restlessness had more to do with the barely tempered chemistry he shared with Addison. No amount of work would fade the memory of his hands on her skin or the feeling of her warmth wrapped around him. Of the taste of her on his tongue. All he wanted to do was kick out his team and have her to himself.

"You look tense, boss." His employee and longtime friend, Aiden Odell, dropped down onto the bench next to him.

The retreat's work portion was over and now the team was relaxing, having a few beers and catching up on personal stuff. But watching Owen flirt with Addison had been enough to make him want to throw something, so he'd gone outside to cool off. It wasn't Owen's fault. Apart from the fact that he was a notorious ladies' man, he had no idea that there was anything at all between Logan and Addison. No one did.

"Just ready to get back to the office. You know numbers aren't my thing."

"You'd be lost without Addison, then." Aiden grinned and swigged his beer. "Hopefully she continues to put up with your shit."

Addison's words echoed in his ears: *Change happens and I might not always be around.*

On Friday night he'd assumed she was talking about her own mortality, but what if she meant that she might want to leave Cobalt & Dane?

"I'm not *that* bad," he said, as if trying to convince himself.

"Man, I'm the only one who's known you long enough

to be able to call you on your crap. Let's be honest. You're difficult as hell."

Logan grunted. "I have high expectations, so what? If people want to work for someone soft, they know where the door is."

"All I'm saying is, this isn't the military. Not everything is life-and-death."

That was the problem, though. People became complacent with their security and then bad things happened. Addison hadn't perceived her email to be a threat and it had gotten her run off the road. If it hadn't been for Rhys, she would have a lot bigger problems right now than a totaled car.

On her request, he'd kept the accident quiet from the rest of their team. But that didn't change what'd happened. Still, what if she *was* thinking of leaving him and their company?

"It's okay to lighten up occasionally, you know, let down that luscious hair of yours." Aiden cracked up when Logan shot him a nasty look.

"Says the guy who should be in a shampoo commercial."

"The ladies love it." Aiden raked a hand through his messy dark curls. "Well, one lady loves it."

"Speaking of crazy hair, how is Quinn?"

Aiden lost his joker smile and he twisted the near-empty beer bottle between his hands. "I'm going to ask her to marry me."

The news hit Logan like a punch to the sternum. "Why the hell would you do that?"

"Because I'm not stupid enough to hide my feelings from her." He shrugged. "She's it for me, Logan. I'm tapping out of the single life."

"I don't even know what to say."

Aiden chuckled and drained the rest of his beer. "How about 'congratulations,' like a normal person would say?"

Logan's eyes were fixed on the distance. Green land spread out for miles around them, the sun growing heavy in the distance. Sometimes he wondered what it would be like to pack up and leave the city behind. It was all too easy to imagine sitting here, drink in hand, with Addison curled up beside him. Her head resting on his shoulder.

You're not allowed to want that. Cobalt & Dane is your life, your purpose. You owe Daniel all that and more.

"I'll congratulate you when she says yes," Logan said with a smirk that belied the confusing swirl of thoughts in his head. "People turn down proposals all the time."

Even a playful swipe couldn't remove the smile from Aiden's face. "Thanks for the vote of confidence."

For a moment Logan envied his friend. But that life wasn't for him. Logan wouldn't be a husband or a dad. He couldn't, not when he was well aware how cruel the world could be. When he knew that grief could crush a man's dreams. Aiden hadn't experienced those things in his life—sure, he'd lost part of his hearing while working for the FBI. But he had a family who loved him, a woman who made him grin like an idiot. Fate hadn't stolen anything from him yet, so he didn't understand how devastating it was to lose someone you cared about.

That's why Logan needed to keep a firm hand on his life, stay in control. Minimize variables and change.

"Is something going on or are you just practicing your resting bitch face?" Aiden nudged him on the shoulder.

"Nah, I'm just ready to head home." He pushed up

from the bench and drained his beer in one long gulp. "I imagine you're ready to get back to your future wife."

"Don't say anything, all right? I want to keep it on the down low."

"Man, the day you catch me talking about weddings will be the day you're obligated as my best friend to shoot me in the head."

"Duly noted."

They abandoned the late-afternoon sun in favor of the cottage's cool, airy kitchen. Addison was sitting on the island bench, her feet swinging back and forth as she chatted with Owen. The heels of her shoes knocked against the wood.

"Probably about time that we get this show on the road," Logan said, tossing his empty beer bottle into the recycling bin.

"Owen's offered to drive me home," Addison said, her cool gaze revealing nothing. Her long blond hair had come out of her ponytail and she wore the hair elastic around her wrist just like she'd done as a teenager. "He said he was heading back to the office to grab something anyway."

Logan's primal instincts roared at him. He had to stop himself from telling Owen to back the fuck away, because that was *exactly* what Addison had complained about the night they arrived at the cottage. And really, he couldn't claim that he didn't trust Owen. The guy was one of his best consultants, a hard worker with far more intelligence than his joker tendencies implied.

"I appreciate it." She smiled and touched Owen's shoulder, all the while keeping her eyes on Logan. "I can't believe the car decided to break down all the way out here. *So* inconvenient."

"It's no problem." Owen patted her hand.

Logan's jaw twitched and he drew a breath.

It's just a lift. And you don't *have the right to tell her who to ride with. Besides, it's not like Owen would make a move.*

Or would he? An image of them flashed into Logan's mind, Owen's hand sliding up Addison's bare leg and catching the hem of her dress, pushing the fabric up. No fucking way.

He cleared his throat. "Actually, Addi, I was hoping we could go through one of those reports before we left. But I don't want to hold the whole team back."

Aiden raised a brow and looked at him like he'd lost his marbles.

"Which report?" she asked with a frown.

Crap. If only he could remember any of the damn spreadsheets that she'd made him look through the last couple of days. "The uhh…cost benchmarking analysis…report."

She cocked her head, her glossy lips pursed. "I'm not sure which one you mean."

Damn her, she wasn't going to let him off the hook that easily. "The one with the…competitor analysis."

"That was just a draft. Surely we don't need to get into that right now. I'll have Renee schedule a time for us to catch up tomorrow."

By this stage the rest of the team had slunk away, sensing the mounting tension between him and Addison. They were known to argue on occasion—each of them as stubborn and fiery as the other. If only his team understood what fueled the fire.

"You're always complaining that I never take any interest in this sort of stuff and now you're saying it can wait?" Guilt streaked through him when her shoulders relaxed and a sheepish smile tugged at her lips.

"You're right, I'm glad you're taking an interest in my stuff for once. I'll tell Owen not to wait."

Could he be any more of a bastard? Not likely.

He watched as she headed over to Owen, her body language so much more relaxed than when she stood with him. The tension had eased out of her lips and she smiled readily. Maybe it would be better if she ended up with someone like Owen, someone who would make her laugh. Someone who would make her life easier.

"If you want to grab a drink later tonight, let me know." Aiden slung his carryall over one shoulder. "That's if you're not too busy going over this report that doesn't exist."

It was Aiden's way of asking if everything was okay. "I won't interrupt your time with Quinn. She'll have my hide if I drag you out after you just got home."

"True. But the offer still stands." Aiden slapped him on the back and then waved to the team.

As the rest of the team filtered out, Addison bade them all individual goodbyes. She was amazing with their employees—firm and yet caring, a true leader who was able to inspire and educate. The problem was that only her own team was as passionate about the numbers side of things. The bean counters and HR folks— or the "fun police" as he'd called them on a number of occasions.

As Owen left, Addison squeezed his arm. They looked good together with their matching blond hair and wide smiles. His gut wrenched. The thought of Addison being with anyone else made him want to hurl.

"So," she said, picking up her laptop from the couch. "You wanted to go over the competitor analysis?"

She padded over to him, barefoot. Her heels lay in a heap by the door and her blue floral dress swished around her knees. The fabric clung to her curves, outlining her breasts and hips in a way that was subtle and yet insanely sexy. He wanted to tear her clothes off with his teeth.

Think of a question about the report.

"Uh, yeah." He rubbed at the back of his neck. "So, what was your overall conclusion about our competitive position?"

She rattled off her answer but he immediately zoned out. Right now, his brain was clogged with too many questions. Who was after Addison and why? What did she *really* expect from him? And what the hell had she meant by her statement that things would change?

"Logan?" Addison waved a hand in front of his face. "I asked if that all made sense."

"Uh yeah, that's great." He nodded and her expression darkened by the second. "So what did you mean before when you said things would change and that you might not always be around?"

"I thought we were supposed to be talking about the report." She planted a hand on her hip. "That's why you asked me to stay back."

"And we just discussed it. Now I want to discuss this."

"It was nothing," she said, turning away from him. She slipped on her shoes and concentrated on the fiddly little straps. "Just a throwaway comment."

"You don't do throwaway comments, Addi. I know that for damn sure."

She was hiding something from him. The more he

thought about what she'd said, the more he suspected that it wasn't simply a product of the accident. Something deeper was going on.

"I was frustrated and tired and…scared." For a second all her confidence and bravado slipped away, and she looked totally vulnerable. "It's a true statement, sure. Things always change—but I didn't mean anything by it."

"You sure about that?"

"I am." She nodded. "Now you can answer a question for me. Why did you really ask me to stay back? Because it sure as hell wasn't for me to repeat the exact same thing I told you earlier today."

"Yeah, about that…" He rubbed his neck again. There was no sense in lying to her now—she'd see right through him. "I wanted to be the one to take you home."

"Logan Matthew Dane, you…" she spluttered. "Are unbelievable."

"I would have thought me doing that was very believable."

She huffed and snapped her laptop shut. "You're also *totally* unapologetic, and I don't know which is worse. What the hell would be wrong with Owen giving me a lift?"

"It's my job."

"To be my taxi driver?" She shook her head and stormed over to where her packed bags sat in a neat pile. As she bent over to stash her laptop away, he caught a flash of blue lace.

God help him. "No, to check your apartment out and make sure it's secure."

"Since when were you going to check my apartment out?"

"Well, obviously I would do that. You've had a threat on your life, Addi. We need to check everything."

"And Owen couldn't have done that? You're always telling me how he's your best consultant and we certainly pay him accordingly. Yet he's not up to the task of checking a few locks all of a sudden?"

Well, damn. What was he supposed to say to that without validating every complaint she'd voiced the other night?

"You didn't want anyone else to know what happened. And besides, I want to do it myself."

Yeah, great. That'll go down like a lead balloon.

She shook her head. "Don't feed me this crap about you wanting to do a security check yourself. I'm fully aware of what you're worried about, and, frankly, it's a little insulting. Even if he was bold enough to make a move, I wouldn't have let him."

Had he been that transparent? He must be losing his touch.

"Do you think I would sleep with you and then jump straight into bed with him?" she continued, her eyes flashing. "Out of the two of us, I'm not the one with *that* track record."

It wasn't possible for him to regret the past any more than he did right now. He'd treated her badly. Reprehensibly.

"Let me drive you home and I'll quickly check out the apartment. Then I'll be out of your hair." He picked up her bags and carried them out to the car.

He might be pushy and overprotective, but he was still her partner. Her friend. And he wasn't going to risk her safety until they knew more about who'd targeted her… and what she meant about things changing.

6

ADDISON SPENT THE duration of the ride home stewing in silence. Her life was a mess. A big, hot, crazy mess. How could she have been so stupid as to let something slip about her not always being around?

She was usually better at controlling her emotions. Now that Logan had gotten a whiff of her secret, he wouldn't let it go. He was a dog with a bone whenever he thought she was hiding something.

Logan was getting into her head and that was *not* a place he should be. They'd been at the cottage for five days and still she couldn't evict the memories of the night they'd had sex from her mind. The memories swirled, gathering steam and distracting her in quiet moments. Like in the dark when she'd lain still, trying desperately to fall asleep.

An aching hunger had gnawed at her, urging her to slip out of her room and into his bed. If it wasn't for the fact that her team was in the cottage with her, she might have.

But Logan was bad news. Bad news for her head and bad news for her heart. What had happened with Owen was a case in point. It was as if his need for control flared up the second there was a whiff of competition. It was a drug for him—he *had* to win. The whole thing was laughable. Owen was a flirt, sure. And gorgeous to boot. But he wasn't interested in her like that; they were friends. Nothing more.

"Are you going to give me the silent treatment the whole way home?" Logan asked.

They'd made it to Manhattan as the sun set. The city was a glittering disco ball around them, and Addison instantly felt safer. There were no deserted roads, and the sheer volume of people comforted her. It was home. She pressed her palm to the passenger window as they wove through the streets.

"I'll take that silence as a yes," he grumbled. "Hate me all you want, that's fine. But I'm still going to be here."

She turned to him, ready to retort, but she didn't have the energy. It was hard to stay mad at someone like Logan. You might not always agree with his behavior—and she certainly didn't—but he lived by a code. So at least he was *consistently* annoying.

The street lights flickered over his profile, etching shadows along his face. They carved out his cheekbones, the harsh angle of his jaw and his straight, perfect nose. Stubble darkened his skin and she had to fight the urge to reach out and touch it.

"You're always here. Like a grumpy shadow." She folded her arms across her chest and snuggled further down into the seat. "Like an antisocial guardian angel."

"Whatever works," he said drily. "Are you going to give me a hard time about checking out your apartment?"

"No." Her lips curved into a sly smile. "Because you're going to order me dinner as well."

"Am I?"

"It's part of the security service. The 'protection and pizza' package."

There was a lull in conversation as they got closer to her place. By the time they'd parked the car and entered her building, Addison was feeling more tired than annoyed. All she wanted was to curl up in bed and bury herself beneath the covers, pretending that she had her life under control.

The night security guard sat behind the concierge desk and Addison waved as they walked past. The man tipped his head in greeting.

"So what exactly are you going to look for upstairs?" she asked as they arrived at the elevators.

"I'll make sure no one has tampered with the locks. It might be worth taking a quick look at your computer as well. I'll have to check in with Rhys, but I've been thinking that if this guy tried to email you at work, he might have tried your personal email, too."

Shit. Her inbox had plenty of evidence that she was planning to move away from Cobalt & Dane, including a conversation with a real estate agent about a potential office space. How on earth was she going to be able to hide that from him?

After what she'd let slip earlier, she'd have to tread carefully. Logan had a nose for secrets.

"Is that necessary tonight?" She feigned a yawn. "The retreat really took the wind out of me. I just want to go to bed."

"I thought you wanted pizza?"

The elevator arrived and he motioned for her to enter ahead of him. A woman with a huge stroller took up most of the space and Addison squeezed herself into the corner to make room for Logan. With his big shoulders and her luggage, there was little room to breathe. As the elevator whooshed upward, she tried not to let herself be intoxicated by his scent. He never wore aftershave, yet he always managed to smell like wood and fresh air.

The elevator stopped and Logan moved to let the mother out. He brushed against Addison, his hand skimming the bare skin of her thigh. Goose bumps rippled across her body, and suddenly she was very much awake. She still wanted to be curled up in bed, but sleep was the last thing on her mind.

"Was that a yes or no on the pizza?" he asked as the doors slid shut, leaving them alone.

"Yes. I'm suddenly quite hungry." Seems she *hadn't* gotten him out of her system.

The air crackled like a fire, heaving with tension. She ran her palms down her dress, trying to slow the beating of her heart. But his magnetic energy was affecting her. Deeply.

"Are you hungry?" she asked.

His eyes were blackened. "Like you would not believe."

She hadn't realized they'd drifted closer to each other until the *ping* of the elevator broke them apart. He juggled the bags and walked into the hallway ahead of her. There was a tightness to his shoulders, a rigidity to his movement. It was clear Logan was also still fighting the attraction between them.

"Addison!" A voice interrupted them as they reached her door. Addison turned to see Mrs. Hollings from down the hall hurrying over. "Wait a second."

Addison stifled a groan. She didn't want to deal with

this right now. The old lady was sweet, but a total busy-body. "Yes, Mrs. Hollings?"

"I'm sorry to interrupt your…" Her birdlike eyes darted to Logan. "Date?"

"You remember Logan Dane, my business partner? He used to work for my father." She forced a smile. "What can we do for you?"

"I wanted to talk to you about something." Mrs. Hollings patted her coiffed silver hair while openly admiring Logan, who looked irritated by the whole thing.

"Go on."

"There was a man asking after you a few days ago. I thought he might have been a suitor calling on you."

Addison frowned. "What was he doing?"

"He was knocking on your door." Mrs. Hollings smiled. "Only he was knocking on the wrong door. He thought you were in the Lims' apartment. But I set him straight."

She looked so proud that Addison didn't have the heart to burst her bubble. "Did he happen to leave a message or a name?"

"No, dear. I asked him if he wanted to because I figured you would be interested. He was very attractive." She tittered.

"What did he look like?" Logan asked, his voice sharp as a gunshot in the quiet hall.

Mrs. Hollings blinked, taken aback by Logan's dark expression. "Oh, well, it was a few days ago…umm. He was tall, dark hair. Very uhhh…" Her hands fluttered at her chest. "Strong-looking."

"Thank you, Mrs. Hollings. I'll be sure to keep an eye out for him." She touched the older woman's shoulder and smiled warmly, trying to ease the worried expression on her face. "I appreciate you looking out for me."

"Oh, of course. Of course." She shuffled back down to her apartment with a wave.

"I hope she realizes she's put you in danger by divulging your address," Logan fumed. "Who does that?"

"She didn't know any better, Logan. Calm down." Addison shoved her key into the lock and opened her front door. "She thought it was a 'suitor' coming to sweep me off my feet."

Logan muttered something under his breath as he shut the door behind them. The apartment was clean and organized, exactly as she'd left it. But she wasn't greeted by the same sense of relief that she usually was upon returning home. Instead, anxious butterflies flittered around in her stomach.

"Is it possible that someone from work came by to drop something off?" she asked without holding much hope. "A tall guy with dark hair could be anyone."

Logan shook his head. "It's not anyone."

"Do you think it's him?" Her heart hammered in her rib cage. When she shut her eyes, she could see him. Well, not him exactly, but the shadowed face that had peered through the window of her car. His voice echoed in her head.

Let me in, you fucking bitch.

Logan's arms were around her and he tucked her head under his chin. "If it is…we can't take any chances. He knows your address."

"I honestly don't understand why this guy is after me."

She'd lived a fairly quiet life, and her role in Cobalt & Dane was strictly on the business side of things. Accounts, payroll, HR. Nothing to anger a dangerous person, at least not that she knew of.

"I don't know, either." His hand brushed the hair from her face. "Why don't you stay at my place tonight?"

"That's not a long-term solution."

"True, but it's late. You're tired. I sure as hell won't sleep if you're here by yourself."

Her cheek rested against the soft cotton of his shirt, the warmth from his skin seeping into her. She pressed a hand to his chest. "What about tomorrow?"

"We'll check the place out more thoroughly then. I'll talk to the building manager and we'll have a look at the security footage. I'll also call the officer who took your statement a few days ago. Hopefully he'll give me access to the gas station footage." He paused. "You'll need to stay with me for a few days, until we have a better handle on this situation."

"Is that a good idea?"

"It's a better idea than you staying here."

Neither of them mentioned the third option of a hotel room. They were in the biggest city in the country; accommodation would not be hard to come by. But the truth was Addison had been well and truly shaken up—as much as she tried not to let it show. If anyone could take care of her security, it was Logan.

So long as you don't mistake his concern over your safety for his caring about you intimately. You are not changing your plans.

"I can set you up in my spare room. There's space in the closet for you to hang your things and you'll have free rein of the place."

Addison wasn't sure if Logan was being gentlemanly by assuming she wouldn't want to be in his bed, or if he was drawing a line in the sand. And she wasn't sure which scenario she preferred.

"Sure." She nodded. "I'll go and pack my things."

At least if they camped out at his apartment she'd have a better chance of keeping her business plans a secret.

THE FOLLOWING DAY Logan sat in his office at the Cobalt & Dane headquarters, wondering what the hell the universe was trying to do to him. He'd spent the night tossing and turning. He'd swung from opposite ends of the emotional spectrum. Battling a desperate desire to sneak into Addison's room and reenact their sexy night together. To beating himself up for thinking about such things when he should be occupied with solving the mystery behind her stalker.

Luckily, he had something to keep his mind busy today. The building manager for Addison's apartment complex was an old friend of her father's. When Addison had moved into the place four years ago, Daniel had made it his business to ensure his little girl was well protected in her new home. Therefore, upon hearing the news that someone was targeting her, the manager had granted Logan immediate access to the security footage for her floor.

Unfortunately, the recording hadn't given him much to work with. A guy in a dark coat and a baseball cap had entered the building by tailgating another resident. Since the concierge appeared to be on patrol at the time of the incident, the man had made it straight up to Addison's floor without anyone vetting him. Logan made a mental note to talk to the building manager about that flaw. The man on the camera had then stopped at the door next to Addison's apartment, though it was difficult to tell what he was doing. Trying to pick the lock, perhaps? The footage also showed Addison's neighbor talking to the man and pointing toward Addison's door.

Logan gritted his teeth. The crazy old bat had no idea what she'd done. What kind of danger she had put Addison in. But as always, Addison had seen the good in a person whereas he'd seen the bad.

A knock interrupted his thoughts. Rhys stood in the doorway of his office. "We got another email."

Logan waved him in. "Close the door behind you. We don't need anyone else to hear about this."

The door shut with a soft *snick* and Rhys took a seat on the other side of the desk. His shoulders were bunched beneath a neat white shirt, and a groove appeared between his eyes. "Shouldn't we involve Addison in these conversations?"

"Just give me the update."

Rhys looked as though he was about to argue but instead he sighed. "The email is from the same address as last time," he said. "It contains more threats, but there was also an attachment. Apparently it's supposed to contain some 'scandalous' pictures of Addison."

Logan's fingers bit into the edge of the desk chair. "Say what?"

"The email sender claims to have nude photos of her. But the attachment looks to be an .exe file, which tells me it's probably a Trojan virus. More than likely, there are no pictures. He's saying whatever he thinks will get her to open the file."

"Why would he want her to open a virus?"

"These types of viruses are designed to grant unauthorized access to a device—in this case, Addison's computer. From there he'd be able to see her emails, watch her browse the internet. He could also skim information like credit card numbers and banking passwords. If she's using the office phone he might even be able to listen to her calls because of the VoIP connection."

Logan's blood ran cold. So this guy wasn't a garden-variety stalker...he was a hacker as well. "But he hasn't gotten access yet?"

"No, I don't believe so." Rhys shook his head. "My team ran an additional scan just in case, and there doesn't appear to be spyware or viruses on her computer or on the network."

"At least one thing has gone right," Logan muttered. "What can you tell me about this guy so far?"

"Not a lot. He's using a generic email address from an online provider. They keep their user information locked up tighter than Fort Knox, so unless we get law enforcement involved we don't have much chance of finding out who this guy is via the email information alone."

"And the chances of the police caring about some faceless person sending a virus is pretty damn slim unless we can connect it to the guy who ran Addison off the road."

Rhys's brows shot up. "Someone ran her off the road? I *thought* the story about her car breaking down seemed odd."

Shit. So much for keeping Addison's secret. "Don't you dare breathe a word of it to anyone. Anyway, all I care about now is what we're going to do next."

"We'll set up a dummy device that's configured to look like Addison's computer. I have an old laptop that will do the trick. Then we open the file in this email and give the hacker access."

"So we can monitor him?"

"Exactly. I can set the dummy up to have access to the internet, but keep it separate from our corporate files. He'll be behind the company firewall, but we'll control his access. We can put the laptop in the DMZ—"

"I don't need the tech talk, Rhys. Just tell me what happens when we give him access."

"We watch him. See what information he's looking for, then do a trace route and follow the bread crumbs. That way we should be able to locate his IP address and use that to find his computer." Rhys flattened his lips into a harsh line. "Then we hunt him down."

"Do it." Logan ran a hand through his hair and tried to stop his mind from racing. "And keep it quiet."

"What about Addison?" Rhys asked, his eyes wary.

"Don't you worry about her. I'll handle it."

The last thing he wanted was for Addison to be any more upset than she was already. He'd bring up the email once Rhys's plan was in place. At least that way she'd know they were doing something to catch this guy.

In the meantime, he wasn't letting her out of his sight.

7

ADDISON JUMPED WHEN her phone rang unexpectedly and shocked her out of her groggy state. Trying to sleep in Logan's spare bed had proved futile last night. Clearly, he didn't believe in investing in a good mattress. The thing had been about as comfortable as a concrete slab. Plus, Logan had padded around his apartment until all hours of the night, his footsteps trampling on any chance she had of slumber.

Part of her had hoped he'd sneak into her room like he had at the cottage. But the other part of her—the part that had gotten a gold star for solidarity—had willed him away. Her life was suddenly far more complicated than she wanted it to be, and the last thing she needed was Logan freaking Dane shaking up her plans.

The more she thought about starting her own company, the more she was certain it was the right move. When her father had convinced her to study business, he'd promised her a seat at the head of the company. A voice. Influence.

But what she'd been too naive to realize at the time was that someone without security expertise would always be a step behind. That her work would only be talked about if something went wrong. Really, it was a behind-the-scenes job—and she *wasn't* a behind-the-scenes kind of person.

Running her own consulting company would give her the best of both words—a way to use the skills she'd honed working for her father *and* an opportunity to sit at the head of the boardroom table. To be taken seriously.

Her phone continued to ring, but Addison couldn't muster up the energy to answer it. Eventually the call diverted to her assistant's phone, and she could hear Renee's perky greeting through the closed door.

Addison checked her email again, as she had done every five minutes for the previous eight hours. It was stupid to think she'd get a nasty message in her inbox, considering the last one had gotten caught in the filter. And Rhys hadn't come to her with any updates. But still, something wasn't right. She could feel it down in her bones.

"Addi?" Renee's voice came through the intercom on her desk phone. "I know you're busy but I've got a gentleman calling from a real estate company. I'm not sure what it's about, exactly."

She snatched the phone from the cradle. "That's okay, put him through." A second later the phone clicked. "Hello?"

"Is this Addison Cobalt?"

"Yes, it is."

"I'm Richard James from Comrade Real Estate. We've been in contact regarding a potential office space in Park Slope?"

She bit down on her lip. The consultant must have gotten her work phone number from her email signature when she'd sent a query. How could she have forgotten to delete it? Stupid, stupid, stupid.

"Yes, Richard. Thanks for your call. I am so sorry to cut you short but I can't speak right now. Would it be okay if I called you back later?"

"Of course, not a problem at all." He read out his number and Addison jotted it straight into the notes section of her phone. After a promise to call him back after she'd left the office, she ended the call.

Crap. All the calls in the office were recorded. Given the nature of their work, they often needed to revisit phone calls between consultants and clients. She had to hope that her move would be all sewn up by the time anyone looked at the call log. The last thing she needed was Logan finding out her plans.

And what will you do if you leave Cobalt & Dane and the stalker comes after you again? How will you defend yourself?

She'd have to cross that bridge when and if she came to it. No one would get in the way of her plans, and she wasn't going to live her life being afraid of every shadow. Her father wouldn't have let some wack job kill his dreams, and neither would she.

Deep down she knew her father would have been proud of her decision to start her own business, even if he'd hated the thought of her being alone in the big bad world.

Addison glanced at the photo on her desk. It was an old one with three smiling faces—father, mother and daughter—taken a few short months before her twelfth birthday. A few short months before heart failure claimed her mother and turned Addison's life upside down. Her father had quit his job as a sergeant major in the army and started Cobalt & Dane with a few ex-military friends. Except it had been only Cobalt Security back then.

Before Logan had come along and taken her place as heir to the company, planting his name alongside her father's on all their letterhead and business cards. All because she'd let her father convince her to take the "safe" route.

Well, she couldn't change the past. But she *could* change the course of her future. Could and would.

As if by some form of magic, Logan appeared in her doorway. "Time to go."

"Go where?" She looked at her phone and realized it was almost seven. How long had she been sitting here staring at the photo?

"Home. Dinner. Wherever."

He was rakishly handsome today, much to her despair. A pair of black jeans and black boots made his legs look strong and lean, while a gray sweater with a short V-neck hugged the muscles in his chest and shoulders. His light brown hair curled around his ears, too long and yet totally perfect. It was the right length to hold on to, to thread between her fingers and pull. Hard.

"Who said I was ready to leave?" She turned back to her computer, needing to look away from him before she forgot that she was supposed to be putting distance between them right now.

"I did. We're going home."

Oh right, *home*. Also known as Logan's place and her temporary prison. "Do you have to be so damn bossy all the time?"

"It's part of my charm." He grinned and she had to bite back a laugh.

"You're totally shameless." She clicked out of her

email and stood, realizing that she was not going to be shaking her sexy shadow anytime soon. And after the week she'd had so far, he was probably the lesser of two evils. "Well, I'm going to need food."

"I've got us a reservation at Maria and Bruno's, that Italian place you said looked nice last week." Renee poked her head into the office and grinned. Her assistant was determined to set Logan and Addison up. If only she knew what they'd done over the weekend. "Logan said you might want to eat out, so I took the liberty."

"That's very…proactive of you."

Renee shrugged, mischief dancing all over her expression. "It's what I do."

Addison stood and smoothed her hands down the front of her black-and-gray shift dress, aware that Logan's eyes were following her every move. Last night, when she'd thrown a few days' worth of clothes into her suitcase, she'd picked this one because she knew how much he liked it.

Two black panels hugged her sides, curving over her hips and legs, making her look tall and slender. The neckline skimmed the boundaries of appropriateness for the office—showing a little cleavage, but not too much. Walking the line between professionalism and sexiness with elegant ease. But the things that made her feel best were the black silk panties she wore underneath. They'd cost more than the dress and were twice as heavenly.

You're a goddamn glutton for punishment, Addison Marie Cobalt. You must love playing with fire.

Perhaps. But her job required her to be confident and in control. And when everything was going to hell she could always rely on her clothes to make her feel powerful. Every little bit helped.

"Fine. Let's head off. Are we driving?"

"I thought we'd walk. It's only a block or two." His eyes lowered slowly, caressing her every curve, until he reached her feet. "Unless your heels are too high."

"Never."

They walked through the office, neither one saying much until they'd made it outside. The sun hadn't yet set, so the air was balmy and pleasant on Addison's bare arms.

"Sometimes I think you choose your outfits to torture me," he said as they walked toward the restaurant.

"Spoken like a true narcissist," she said, smirking. "Not everything is about you."

The street was still busy with office workers, suited men and women bustling in all directions around them. The traffic trudged past, steady but slow. Addison dodged a woman charging past in the opposite direction.

"I suppose your dumb boyfriends might fall for those quippy lines," he said. "But I know better than that."

Her lips curled into a smile but she wouldn't give him the satisfaction of admitting he was right.

"Keep convincing yourself of that."

"Look me in the eye and tell me I'm wrong." His hand snaked around her waist as he guided her out of the path of a couple coming in the other direction. "Tell me you don't think about me when you wriggle into those tight little dresses."

She resisted the urge to melt against him, but instead concentrated on putting one foot in front of the other. Her heels clicked against the pavement. "Is it wrong to want some appreciation?"

"Not if you own it."

"Fine. I like it when you look at me." She'd gotten

hooked on his attention from the moment he'd seen her not as a child, but as a woman. "So sue me."

"How about we have a drink before things get litigious?"

They pulled up in front of the restaurant and Addison cursed Renee under her breath. The restaurant screamed "date" with its intimate tables for two and gentle candle-lit atmosphere. She was hardly going to be able to concentrate on keeping carnal thoughts from her mind in this setting.

"After you." He held the door for her.

They were seated right away, at a table tucked into the back corner of the dining area. No doubt Renee had requested it. She made a mental note to give her assistant a few "guidelines" on booking an appropriate location for a work dinner. Because that's what this was—work.

Yeah right. And you think he *needs to stop bullshitting himself.*

"This seems…" Logan scanned the room. "Cozy."

"I did not suggest this to Renee as an option for dinner. I simply said the dessert menu looked good." She shook her head. "That's what I get."

Logan appeared unconvinced, but he didn't say anything further on the matter as the waiter arrived to take their orders.

"I've arranged to have Aiden help me at your place tomorrow," he said as the waiter left. "I trust him to keep the situation under wraps. We'll do a sweep of the apartment and change the locks. You can be there to supervise, if you like."

"You're inviting me to my own house," she said drily. "How considerate."

"It has to be done this way." Logan rolled his shoulders back and she tried not to stare as the soft sweater stretched across his pecs. "So, was that a yes or a no?"

"Yes, of course I want to be there."

If she was there, she'd be able protect her plans. She could convince Logan she was perfectly capable of handing her laptop over to Rhys by herself, which would give her time to dump the files onto a USB and wipe them off her computer.

Maybe you should come clean and tell him?

Sneaking around was hard work, but she knew what Logan would say. He'd try to convince her to stay, and she didn't want to be vulnerable to his influence the way she'd been to her father's all those years ago.

Her dad hadn't wanted her anywhere near the business at first, hoping to shield her from the dark side of his world. But doing her father proud by joining the family business was the only wish she'd had as young girl. Then precious Logan had come along and taken up residence by her father's side. She should have hated him for that. She'd *wanted* to hate him on some level.

But her brain and her heart never seemed to agree where Logan was concerned.

"You got serious all of a sudden," he commented, his eyes searching her face.

"I was thinking about Dad. I can't believe it's been two years."

"Sometimes I walk into your office hoping I'll see him behind that desk." Logan's voice was almost lost under the sound of conversation from the adjacent tables. "It's like I forget he's gone, just for a moment."

"And then it all comes rushing back, doesn't it?" She swallowed at the sudden lump in her throat.

"Yeah."

Logan hadn't talked much about his feelings over losing her father, but she knew he'd taken it as hard as she had. Over the years she'd gleaned bits and pieces about Logan's past; she'd learned that he'd lost his mother like she had. That he'd left the military and that he didn't get along with his father, but she wasn't exactly sure why. If she pressed him for more details, her questions were usually silenced with a glare sharp enough to cut bone.

"Sometimes you sound just like him," Logan said. "Especially when you jam the copier and swear at it as if it can hear you."

"He hated that damn machine." She smiled at the memory.

Her father had generally been cool, calm and collected…but not when it came to technology. A self-confessed Luddite, he'd eschewed the internet when it had first come along, had refused to get a smartphone and had a tendency to break things out of frustration when he couldn't figure out how to operate them.

"I was sure I'd turn up at the office one day to find that he'd taken a baseball bat to it." The candlelight caught Logan's dark eyes, the flame reflecting in their depths.

"I'm glad I managed to inherit such great qualities from him," she said with a laugh.

"You got plenty from him, Addi. Your fiery spirit, your ability to think on your feet. And your fierce loyalty, you definitely got that from him."

Fierce loyalty. Would he still think her loyal when she up and left?

"Got that snarky quick wit from him, too," Logan added.

For a moment he looked lost. Haunted. It was an expression she saw on his face occasionally—when his mind drifted to dark things that he never wanted to talk about. Now he looked so much like that lost twenty-something boy who'd turned up at her father's office with a chip on his shoulder and a permanent scowl. She'd realized later that he was scowling at himself, not at those around him.

"I know you think I'm a pushy bastard, but I won't ever stop trying to protect you." Logan gazed at her with an intensity that made her heartbeat kick up a notch. "I sat with your dad at the hospital, watched him fade away, and I *promised* him I would keep you safe. You were more precious to him than anything in the world."

She blinked back the tears prickling her eyes. God, she missed her father so much it hurt her to breathe. People kept telling her that time would heal all wounds, but she found that grief came in waves. Like an ocean of longing and pain lapping at her—sometimes gently and other times with the ferocity of a tsunami.

"I haven't kept many promises in my life, but I won't break that one. No matter how much you hate me for it."

"I don't hate you for it," she said. "I just want to live my own life."

The urge to open up to Logan, to unburden herself of the secret, tugged at her again. But it wasn't the right thing to do. She might trust him with her body and her safety, but she certainly didn't trust him with her dreams, or her heart.

LOGAN REACHED FOR the glass of scotch that the waiter had delivered. The single ice cube bobbed in the rich amber liquid, clinking against the glass as he raised it to his lips. The smoky warmth soothed him, quieted the demons.

He had no idea why he was getting into this with Addison now, but some part of him felt the need to connect with her on a deeper level than their usual to and fro.

She took a sip of her wine. "On the upside, no further contact from my stalker."

She tried to make light but Logan cringed inwardly. Keeping the second email to himself was the right decision, at least until they had a plan in place that would make Addison feel safer.

"Call me crazy, but some days I want to be the girl who falls in love with a guy at the grocery store and then grows old with kids running around her feet." She opened her mouth as if she was about to say something else, but then she snapped it shut as their food arrived at the table.

"Why do you think you'll find Mr. Perfect at the grocery store?" he asked as he tucked into his pasta.

Addison blew on the steam curling up from her dish, her glossy lips pursing in a way that made Logan shift in his seat. Those lips had been at the center of many a fantasy of his. They were perfect—full, ripe. Naturally pink.

"I don't know." She stuck her fork into the mound of spaghetti and twirled. "Isn't that the kind of thing you see in the movies? The girl is picking out the perfect orange and then she turns and bumps into the man of her dreams. It's sweet."

"It's fiction."

"And I can't indulge my imagination? It's better than reality."

"Reality isn't all bad." At least not the reality of their night together.

Damn, it'd been so good that he couldn't go three minutes without his mind drifting into fantasyland. If only he could take Addison to bed and stay there. Forget about his job, forget about his promises. Forget about everything but the silken feel of her skin under his palms.

"Reality is complicated." She sighed. "And I don't like complicated."

Which was exactly why they'd never work as a couple. He was the definition of complicated—fucked-up family, abandonment issues and a hero complex. Not exactly a rom-com catch.

Not exactly a catch by anyone's standards.

He cleared his throat. "Me either."

"Why do we make things hard on ourselves, Logan? And I mean the royal we, as in people in general." Her tongue darted out to capture the sauce clinging to the corner of her lip. "For example, we had sex and now both of us are dancing around it like it's some big bad thing."

Logan raised a brow. "We are?"

"Yes, we are. Tell me, did you consider coming into my room last night?"

He contemplated lying, but Addison was always good at seeing through his poker face. "Yes."

"But you didn't. Why not?"

Because I'm worried that I'll fuck things up and dishonor the promise I made to your father.

A strand of golden hair had escaped her updo. It fell against her cheek, catching the candlelight and looking like spun gold. Everything about her was so perfect, so angelic. It would be wrong to inflict his messed-up life on her.

"Well?"

He sighed. "I'm trying to preserve our relationship."

"And why would sex make that difficult? Are you

planning on using me and then shacking up with some-one else…again?" Her lips were pressed into a flat line.

God, if ever there was an opportunity for him to take something back, that would be it. The shock of losing Daniel had driven a crack right through him. It'd formed a gaping hole so dark and so ugly that he'd filled it the only way he knew how. With drinking and sex and run-ning away.

Only he'd run away emotionally, rather than physi-cally. He'd pushed Addison away—horrified that she might finally see how vulnerable he was deep down—by finding someone else to share his bed. Someone he didn't care about.

This was why he would never deserve her. No matter how many times he atoned for his sins.

"No," he said. "I won't be repeating that mistake."

"Good." She sighed. "Look, I know you're attracted to me. I'm attracted to you…why are we dancing around it so much? It's not as if I'm expecting you to give me the white picket fence dream. I know that's not you."

"Because you deserve the guy at the grocery store. You deserve the happy ending."

"That can wait. Besides, we agreed that we wouldn't get emotionally involved. No expectations, remember?"

Under the table he felt something brush his leg. Her foot was tracing a line up the inside of his pants. Was she going to take it further? Right here?

"Right now I want a different kind of ending."

Holy shit. Logan almost knocked his drink over when her foot migrated into his lap, nudging his cock until it stirred. He was hard in an instant.

"Addison," he said, his eyes darting to the table next to him. The other diners appeared to be none the wiser of their little game. "If you keep that up I'm not going to be able to get out of this restaurant without poking someone's eye out."

She continued to rub him, and his cock swelled in response. "We can slip out the back."

His mind whirred. "Out the back?"

"Into the alley."

"It's not safe, and if it *is* safe that means they'll have cameras." He shook his head, trying to separate rational thought from the part of his brain that wanted the pleasure she was offering. "I'm not sharing you with anyone."

"Boring," she teased. "You're always so sensible."

"One of us has to be." She didn't know that he was balancing on a knife's edge. "I'm not going to risk you getting mugged with your skirt up around your waist, either."

"That would be quite a story." A smile quirked on her lips. "But I bet we don't make it home before you start tearing my clothes off."

"You think I'm that weak?"

"No. I think *I'm* that good at pushing your buttons."

"Those are fighting words." He reached under the table and captured her foot. The silk stockings that covered her legs were smooth in his palm. "You want to fight me, Addison?"

"Very much so." Her eyes were wide, dark. Excitement lit her cheeks.

He rubbed his thumb over her ankle, tracing the delicate bone in circles. "What's the wager?"

"Full control for the next three days. If I win, you'll fix up my apartment and then leave me to my business unless *I* ask for your protection." She folded her hands neatly on the table. "And you have to tell everyone at work that I'm a better boss than you are."

A smile twitched on his lips. "And if I win?"

"You can boss me around as much as you like. I'll do anything you want without complaint."

Her words rocketed through him, scorching him from the inside out. "Anything?"

"Whatever your wicked heart desires."

8

ADDISON'S THUDDING HEARTBEAT filled her ears as she waited for Logan to take the bait. His hands were on her foot, rubbing her calf, while she slowly stroked his cock.

She hadn't intended to seduce him in a restaurant full of strangers when the evening started, but something about the way he'd opened up…it had gotten to her. He might not be her "grocery store guy" like in the movies, but he cared about her on some level. That much she knew. And if she wasn't expecting a happily-ever-after from him then what was the harm in indulging in a long-held fantasy? Especially if she could use it to her advantage by getting him out of her apartment.

Even last night—torn as she'd been about the way he was behaving—she knew damn well that if he'd walked through her bedroom door she would have welcomed him with open arms. Her body craved him, and so long as she kept her heart locked up, that wasn't a problem. Addison was sick of being at the mercy of Logan's whims—he wanted her, then he pulled away. Hot, cold, hot, cold.

Like a goddamn Katy Perry song.

So it was time for her to take charge.

"No expectations?" he clarified.

"Only that I'll win."

"Doubtful. I hope you know it's dangerous to give full control to a guy like me," he said. "You never know what I'll do with it."

Ain't that the truth.

"I want to take a few more risks in my life," she replied. "I'm tired of being the good girl."

His eyes narrowed. "Fine."

"Fine?"

"I accept your dare."

"Good." She reached for her wine and then drained it in one long gulp. "I just need to use the restroom before we go."

When she returned, they abandoned their half-eaten meal and Logan threw some bills onto the table. A thrill ran through Addison's body as they wove through the now-crowded restaurant. Logan's hand landed possessively at her waist, his presence radiating behind her.

Nobody gave them a second glance, and that made her all the more excited. Like they shared a secret. A naughty secret.

Addison wasn't usually the instigator of such things. The two times she'd slept with Logan it had been spontaneous, driven by some deeper emotion that had fought its way out. With other men—the few there had been—she'd let them take the lead because she'd always been a little anxious, a little unsure. But with Logan she felt powerful and sexy and fierce.

She felt safe.

He would never harm her, not physically. Even if she gave him full control. He would never push her to do something she didn't want to do. Knowing that, she could make this bet. Though she was confident she'd win.

After all, if she could get him hard as stone with just her foot, then she could bring him to his knees when all her faculties were at her disposal.

"Are you curious about what I'll make you do when I win?" he asked as they stepped out into the balmy night air.

"I don't usually spend much time pondering the impossible, but I'll indulge you this once." She smiled. "What have you got planned? Some role play? Maybe you want me to dress up and wait on you hand and foot? Or maybe you want to tie me up and tickle me mercilessly?"

His jaw twitched.

"Or *maybe*," she said, linking her arm through his and leaning in close to his ear, "you want to bend me over your knee and spank me until my ass is good and pink."

She let her lips brush the sweet spot next to his ear. As much as the teasing was meant for him, the image of her folded over his lap—his hand swatting her—made her blood fizz.

For a moment she thought she had him—his eyes squeezed shut and he exhaled a long breath through his lips. He barely moved except for the slight bob of his Adam's apple.

But Logan Dane wouldn't go down on the first blow. Anticipation skittered through her.

"I was thinking I'd get you on your knees," he said, his composure back in place. His eyes were intense, shadowed. "To start."

"Yes?" she breathed.

"You see, my filing cabinets are quite low. So you'll

need to be kneeling so you can rearrange them properly."
He burst out laughing when she glared at him. "Oh come
on, Addi. You didn't think I'd bend that easily, did you?"

"You might be laughing now, but you're at risk of
breaking a zipper." They stopped at a corner, waiting for
the pedestrian sign to change. She leaned in, pretending
to peck him on the cheek, but instead she slipped her
hand down and felt for him.

Just as she'd suspected, hard as a rock.

"A lucky guess," he muttered.

"Luck has nothing to do with it."

The sky was dark now, affording them a little more
cover. They had a good four blocks before they reached
Logan's apartment, which should be ample time for her
to work him into a frenzy. She was high on the competition. High on the idea of getting him to bow to *her*
will for once.

The lights changed and they crossed the road. "So,
of *all* the things you could possibly get me to do, your
mind went to filing? That's sad."

He chuckled and the sound rippled through her. "I
had to think of something that would calm me down.
Paperwork seemed the best option."

"I bet I could make it interesting."

"You're already going to lose one bet tonight. I'd be
wary about taking on another."

"Okay, Mr. Smarty-Pants. If you're going to be like
that, I won't play nice anymore."

She reached into the pocket on the inside of her bag
where she'd cheekily stashed her panties after returning
from the restroom back at the restaurant. Initially, her
plan had been to surprise him closer to home on a quiet
little side street and let him feel his way to that discovery.

But he was playing hard to get.

Her fingertips brushed the expensive silk and she toyed with the little ribbon that held the sides together. As they rounded a corner, she pulled the panties out and stealthily tucked them into his hand.

"What the hell?" he said, looking at her and then dropping his eyes down to his hand. "Christ, Addison. Are these what I think they are?"

"If you think they're a pair of Agent Provocateur *ouvert* panties, then you're correct." The style was her favorite, with little cutouts and fiddly ribbons that made her feel like a million bucks. "Spoiler alert, I'm wearing the matching bra."

He stuffed the panties into his pocket but not before she saw him rub the silk between his fingers and his nostrils flared. His cool was slipping.

"I figured I'd save you the trouble of getting them off. They're delicate and I didn't want you to rip them." She slipped his hand over her shoulder and turned her face up to his. "Save your teeth for me."

He swore under his breath, his arm tightening around her. "You're going to be the death of me, Cobalt."

"At least you'll die happy, *Dane*."

"Die happy and go straight to hell. Sounds about right." He grinned at her with a rakish devil-may-care expression.

It wasn't often that he looked at her that way. Since he'd barreled into her life he'd been moody and dark, any joking or teasing undercut with a current of tension. Restraint.

"If everyone got sent to hell for having great sex, then I'd be happy to go there, too. It'd be quite the party."

"So it's *great sex*, huh?"

Heat crept into her cheeks, and she hid it by resting her head against his shoulder. "What would you call it?"

"Words aren't my thing."

They crossed another road and his apartment building loomed ahead. A quiet alley was a few feet off to their right, so she took his hand and pulled him toward the shadows. "Show me then."

The alley was little more than an exit for the underground parking of one of the apartment towers on the block. On the other side was a fence that sectioned off a children's playground. It was dark, but anyone looking closely would be able to see them.

She led Logan past the parking lot entrance and into the shadows. "It's just us now."

Heart hammering, she pulled him close and wedged herself between the hard muscle of his chest and the brick building. Her hands went to his pecs, sliding up until they curled around his jaw. Rough stubble scratched her palms and she tugged him closer. The moment his lips hit hers, she was lost. Obliterated.

His tongue pushed between her teeth and he pinned her against the wall. The hard jut of his cock sent her brain into meltdown. All she wanted was to feel him inside her.

"Addi," he moaned as he ground himself against her. He yanked her leg over his hip and slid his hand up over the band of her thigh-high stocking until he cupped her bare ass.

The cool night air caressed her naked skin. She'd never done anything so wicked as this, so brazen. But it felt good to step out of her shell, to take charge of her life. To throw caution to the wind.

Logan's hand skirted her hip, his fingertips tracing

a red-hot trail to her sex. Her whole body was alight. "God, you feel good."

A car came out of the parking lot then, its headlights brushing over the alley and narrowly missing them. For a moment everything was light and then they were dropped into shadows again. For some reason, the realization that they could be caught made Addison even more excited.

"Do you know exactly what I want to do to you right now?" Logan's breath was hot against her cheek as his fingers brushed her.

"What?"

"I want to feel you come against my hand." He circled her clit, gently at first. Lightly teasing. "I want those beautiful thighs to tremble."

Her head lolled back against the brick. "Yes."

She had him right where she wanted him. Victory would taste so sweet, but she wouldn't dare interrupt him. Orgasms first, gloating second.

"I want your whole body to shake with pleasure." His teeth scraped down her neck, his fingers increasing the pressure between her legs.

"Logan," she sighed.

Her tummy fluttered, pleasure flooding through her as her sex clenched. Voices floated down the alley as a couple walked past the parking lot. She clamped a hand over her mouth but Logan didn't slow down. The couple kept walking, none the wiser to what was going on a few feet away.

"You want to play games, Addi?" His voice was as rough as the bricks behind her. Hard. Edgy. "You know I love to win."

A smile curved on her lips. "Do you?"

He stroked her in soft circles, picking up the pace as her breath hitched. She was so close her heart hammered in her chest, but he held her on edge. Balancing her pleasure so that she hovered at the entrance to nirvana—release just out of reach.

"I do and I *am*. Which is why this is going to feel even better." He slid a finger inside her, all the while grinding the heel of his palm against her sensitive clit.

White light exploded behind her eyelids and she bit into her hand to keep from crying out. The world seemed to slide from beneath her feet and she was floating. Falling. Flying.

Her knees shook but he held her up, allowing her to loop her arms around his neck while she found her strength.

"I guess I can order you to carry me home now?" she said, her eyes fluttering open.

"Wrong." He pressed his lips to her forehead. "We're walking to my place now and then I'll be ready to claim my prize."

"You've already lost." She straightened and tugged her skirt down, fiddling with the bands of her stockings.

"No, I haven't. The bet was whether or not we'd make it home without me tearing your clothes off." He grinned. "And luckily for me you removed the one piece of clothing that I needed off."

Her mouth fell open, but her brain was too lust-addled to form a comeback.

"I would say the pleasure's all mine, but I don't think that's the case." He grabbed her hand and pulled her away from the wall. "Come on, time's a-wasting. I'm ready to start bossing you around."

IF SHE WANTED to start taking more risks, then it was better that she take them with him rather than with someone who might not have her best interests at heart. At least that's what Logan was telling himself. Because really, did bringing her to orgasm in a city alleyway count as looking out for her best interests?

"If I had known you were such a cheater I wouldn't have made the bet with you," she said, huffing as they walked onto the street.

The sound of her heels clicking against the pavement made his blood thrum. "Don't be mad at me. You were the one who didn't think the bet through."

"'Tearing someone's clothes off' is a figurative term." She narrowed her eyes at him. "I simply meant that you wouldn't be able to keep your hands off me."

"Then you should have said that. I'm a literal guy."

"You're something, all right," she muttered.

Bringing her pleasure made him feel as powerful as a god. At the same time, he swallowed down the burgeoning guilt as it climbed up his throat, threatening to strangle him if he wasn't careful. He wouldn't hurt Addison as he'd done before by running away the morning after.

He would need to process their situation, roll it over in his mind so that he could rationalize his behavior.

But he wouldn't inflict that kind of pain on her again.

And you believe tomorrow you'll both go on your merry ways as if nothing happened? You've been thinking about her constantly since the weekend. That won't change.

Maybe not. But nothing—with the exception of her putting on the brakes—would stop him from having her now. Not guilt, not the ghosts of his past. Not his own fucked-up issues.

He wanted her. And for the first time, he was going to let himself revel in having her.

They arrived at his building and he pulled his key card out of his wallet. "You know my prize kicks in the second I walk through those doors." He reached for her hand. "And I've been walking for four blocks with a very stiff cock because of you."

The annoyance slipped from her features, replaced by vulnerability and naked excitement that lit up her dark eyes. "Are you going to punish me?"

"You're going to enjoy it. So I'm not certain it can be classed as punishment."

"Well," she said, plucking the key card out of his hand, "we'd better get inside, then."

"Does this mean you're going to be a gracious loser?" he asked as they walked through the quiet foyer.

"Hardly."

The man behind the security desk gave them a brisk nod, but Logan didn't miss the way the other man's eyes lingered on Addison. Instinctively, he slipped an arm around her shoulder and pulled her close. He wasn't sure what the caveman-style display said about him—not likely anything positive.

So what else is new?

She stayed close to him as they rode the elevator up, her fingers interlaced with his and her thumb stroking the ridges of his knuckles. The sensation made his chest clench. They'd been here before.

When her father had died, they'd sat together outside the hospital room. Holding hands. Silent. She didn't cry—rather, she'd sat like a statue, shock freezing her body. He'd touched her in this same way, a gentle brush of his thumb over her knuckles. A small movement, private. Meant to comfort.

Then he'd blown it all to hell by treating her like shit.

"Addi?" He leaned his head against hers his mind scrambling for the right words to say.

"Yeah?"

The feeling was there, the desire to tell her that he was sorry. But the words clogged his throat. God, he sucked at the personal stuff.

He swallowed. "I hope you're prepared for an ass-swatting."

"I'm all yours for the next few days, so do with me what you will." A tremor ran through her. "Just don't hurt me too bad, okay?"

"Addi, my aim is to make you feel good."

I never mean to hurt you.

The elevator dinged and they walked down the corridor toward his apartment. "I want to make you feel good, too," she said quietly.

"You do, baby. No doubt about that."

He dug his key out, fumbling with it as he tried to open the door. What the hell was wrong with him? He was nervous all of a sudden. Anxious at the thought of what would happen once he got her inside his apartment. Desperate to get his hands on her again.

Finally, he got the door open. If Addison noticed his nerves she didn't say anything. But Logan could practically taste the excitement fizzing on his tongue. He held the door for her and she walked past, her hands trailing across his thighs. Skirting the bulge in his pants.

"You're such a tease," he said.

She lifted a delicate shoulder as she discarded her bag. "Where do you want me?"

"So it's like that, is it? Straight down to business."

"I figured you wouldn't want to waste time."

She stood in front of him, a few blond hairs escaping her neat updo. They were the only sign of their "detour" on the way home. The rest of her was polished and poised, as always. He stuck his hand into his pocket and pulled out the panties. When she'd given them to him before, he'd only felt the silk and ribbons.

But now, in the privacy of his apartment, he could take his time to appreciate them. The panties were black—a mixture of high-quality silk, bound with ribbons and a slight frill that would have curved around her ass. Strategic cutouts were designed to show as much as they concealed. Teasing without giving away the goods entirely.

"I can't wait to see what the rest of this set looks like." He closed the distance between them and her breath stuttered in the quiet.

"Can I show you?" Her hands went to the zipper that ran down the side of her body, but he stopped her.

"No. That's my job."

He drew the zipper down slowly, letting the dress gape open to reveal a hint of black silk at her bust. The stark contrast with her fair skin made his blood pulse hotter. She shrugged out of the dress and it pooled at her feet. Holding her hand, he helped her step out of the fabric.

Logan let out a long, low whistle of appreciation. "Christ, Addison."

Her lips twitched. "You like?"

His gaze swept over her, drinking in the bare skin and black finery. Sheer black stockings stopped midthigh, capped with thick bands of lace. The pencil-thin heels made her look even taller and leaner. And the bra—if you could even call it that—forced her breasts up and out, the creamy mounds all but spilling over the tiny, semisheer cups.

"'Like' doesn't even begin to describe it." He smoothed his palms up and down her waist, his hands flaring out over her naked hips. "Turn around."

She obeyed. Her ass was round and ripe as a peach, perfectly pale and unmarked.

Not for long.

"Put your hands on the couch." His voice didn't sound as though it belonged to him anymore; he was in a dream state. "Spread your legs."

She moved into position, bracing herself on the back of the couch. God, she looked so beautiful laid out like that. Blood rushed in his ears, his body primed and very ready for her.

"You've got me so wound up," he said. "I want to be inside you so bad I can barely see straight."

"Then do it." She gazed back at him over her shoulder. "I'm all yours."

He drew a fingertip down the length of her spine and she bit her bottom lip. Her strangled moan sent a surge of lust through him.

"Say it again," he growled.

Goose bumps rippled across her, peppering her perfect white skin. Her lips parted. "I'm all yours," she whispered.

If only that was true. For now, he would have to forget the past, forget his promises. Forget everything but how much he wanted her. And how good he was going to make her feel.

9

ADDISON SHIFTED IN her heels, the silence unnerving her. Why was Logan hesitating? Was he going to pull away and leave her hanging? Her stream of questions was cut short when a soft hand landed on her hip.

"I've got you for three days. Three whole fucking days, and I want to take full advantage." His lips pressed against her spine and he slowly kissed his way down it until he stopped above her backside. "What do you say if you want me to stop?"

"I won't," she breathed. "I won't want you to stop."

"What do you say, Addi? Pick a word." He stilled. "I'm not giving you anything until I hear it."

She wanted to squeeze her thighs together, anything to stop the throbbing. Anything to get some friction. "Paperwork," she said, grinning into the fabric of his couch. "That's my word."

Behind her, a deep, throaty laugh rumbled. "That *will* make me stop in my tracks."

Before she could come up with a retort, his hands were between her legs, smoothing up and down the inside of her thighs. Tracing her. Learning her. They brushed high, but not high enough. The throbbing intensified.

She shut her eyes and silently begged for him to take the next step. The buildup would bury her if she didn't get what she needed soon. But Logan was stringing things out, relishing his power over her. The sound of a zipper being drawn down ratcheted up her heartbeat. Something soft hit the floor. *Yes, yes, yes.*

His palm came down onto her ass with a sharp *crack*. "Oh!" The cry flew out of her mouth before she could stop it. After all that waiting, she hadn't been sure what to expect.

A gentle touch followed, his hand rubbing the stinging spot in circles. Soothing. Preparing. Warmth radiated through her, the sharp pain fading quickly. Another swat followed on the other cheek, and her body jolted.

"You're pink already," he said, his voice strained. "So pretty and pink."

Another hand came down. Addison's whole body hummed in response, delicious heat flaring in her like a struck match. *Smack, smack, smack!* Her sex ached for him; it clenched with each hit. His hands smoothed over her, helping to spread the tingling throughout her body.

"I can't wait anymore." His hands left her and a moment later she heard foil tearing.

Then he spun her around, picked her up and planted her on the back of the couch. When he finally pushed inside her it was sweet relief. She arched, tilting her hips to let him go as deep as possible. Pain flared as his fingers bit into her tender backside, holding her firm while he thrust into her.

"So tight." He pressed his face against her hair. "So soft."

Addison wrapped her legs around his waist and her arms around his neck, clinging to him like she was falling and he was the hand that could save her. In that moment he was the only thing tethering her to earth. The only thing she cared for.

"You make me crazy," he muttered as he brought his lips to hers. Peppering kisses all over her.

"You *are* crazy," she panted.

Her head lolled back, but he fisted his hand in her hair and yanked her face up, crushing his lips down to hers. His tongue drove its way into her mouth and she moaned into him. Every one of her senses was overloaded—from the warmth on her skin to the sound of his labored breath as he thrust into her. The scent of sweat and something uniquely him. The taste of scotch on his lips. She wanted to absorb it all.

"Only when I'm with you." He palmed her breast through her bra, rolling her nipple between his thumb and forefinger until she writhed in pleasure. "Always when I'm with you."

The words pushed her closer to the edge. In his arms she felt as though she mattered, as though they were equals. Her whole body clenched as he increased the pace, practically lifting her off the couch while he slammed into her.

"I'm so close." She ground the words out. "Please, Logan. Please."

Their bodies were mashed together, tight and hot. Slick with perspiration. He angled her back to increase the friction and a moment later she exploded with sweet release. Her muscles clamped down on him and he followed her over the edge, saying her name over and over like a prayer.

SOMETIME LATER, AFTER they'd showered and gotten lost in each other again, they sat on Logan's balcony. Addison had raided his freezer and found an unopened pint of Ben & Jerry's Cherry Garcia, which she'd claimed. She dug her spoon into the chunky dessert and popped some into her mouth.

"You never struck me as an ice cream guy," she said, licking the spoon clean. "Especially not chocolate cherry flavored."

"It's yours, remember?" He interlaced his fingers behind his head and stretched back. "We were working on a board presentation a few months ago. You said my cupboards made you sad."

"And you never opened it? Geez, ice cream doesn't last longer than a day or two in my freezer." She chuckled. "I guess some girls want to leave a toothbrush and I just want something sweet."

"You've always had a thing for sweets. Remember that time we went to Magnolia Bakery? You begged me to go because you'd heard the older girls at school talking about when they'd seen it on *Sex and the City*."

"And Dad wouldn't let me watch it. I was so mad at him." She sucked on her spoon. "But then you took me there and bought every little cake that I pointed at."

The memory made her smile. Gruff twentysomething Logan in his combat boots, shoulder-length hair and all-black outfit and a sheltered, seventeen-year-old Addison who still hadn't grown out of her pink phase. What a strange pair they'd made. Eventually she'd grown up and he'd mellowed out until they found a middle ground. But he'd looked out for her from the beginning, even if it was only to smooth over her teenage drama with her dad.

"I've never seen such a small person devour so much

cake in all my life. I think I blew half my paycheck on that trip."

"Worth it. That was some damn tasty cake."

Addison closed her eyes and let the cool breeze brush over her skin. The warm weather was gathering steam and soon the city would turn into an oppressive, sticky mess like it did every summer. They probably only had another week or two before it hit.

"We should get to bed," Logan said, looking down at his watch. "I want to get an early start tomorrow so we can knock off after lunch and check out your apartment."

"Can't I just sit here and pretend everything is normal?" Her eyes scanned the glittering skyline.

Sometimes Addison would sit on her own balcony and wonder about all the people scurrying through the city, small as ants, while she sat and watched from above. Who were they? What were they doing? Where were they going? It made her feel small, but in a good way. Like her issues were only a speck of dust.

"Everything will *be* normal, once we figure out who this guy is. But until then, we can't ignore reality." He stood and held a hand out to her. "Come on, I'll even let you pick which side of the bed you want."

"Is that your way of asking me to stay with you tonight?" She slipped her hand into his, relishing his strength as he hoisted her to her feet.

"I'm not asking, Addi. I'm telling. Remember our deal?" He motioned for her to walk ahead of him. "Now get that precious ass inside before I get the idea to spank you again."

The next morning Logan woke early. He wasn't used to sharing his bed, nor to being woken up in the middle of

the night by wandering hands and muffled sleep-talking.
But stroking Addison's hair until she'd calmed enough
to fall into a deeper slumber had dislodged something
in his chest. Almost as if a piece of the wall around his
heart had broken away.

*And what good will that piece do floating around in
your chest? It'll carve you up.*

He'd dressed quietly, taking only a moment to watch
the goddess in his bed. Her blond hair had spilled over
his navy sheets, and a pale hand hung over the edge of
the mattress while she slept facedown on his pillow. She
had taken up the whole bed, her limbs stretched out like
a starfish.

They'd both grown up as only children, so sharing
wasn't something that came naturally to either of them.
But he liked that about her. She wasn't afraid to make
her presence known; she didn't shrink into a corner or
stand at the edge of a crowd.

Addison was nobody's wallflower.

Unable to bring himself to wake her, he slipped out.
The fresh air would do him good before he started his
workday, and he didn't know if Addi needed a coffee first
thing. She'd made one at the cottage. Better, in his mind,
to burn a few dollars on a drink she may not want than
potentially face the wrath of an uncaffeinated woman.

He walked back from his favorite coffee spot with
a latte for her and an Americano for him. The city was
starting to wake. People filtered out of their homes onto
the tree-lined street, dressed in suits and all manner of
fashionable things. Despite growing up in such a cosmo-
politan city, Logan had little time for fashion...unless it
was related to Addison's lacy underthings.

A wave of lust washed over him. Last night he'd let

himself go in a way that was truly foreign. He'd been unable to hold back. Unable to rein in his passion and desire. The fact that she'd trusted him enough to hand him the keys to the kingdom unsettled him to his core. He didn't deserve it.

But now he'd tasted the forbidden fruit and he was hungry for more.

A woman exiting his building held the door for him and he nodded to her with a quick smile. He'd lived in this building for four years and he didn't have a relationship with a single one of his neighbors. He knew plenty *about* them, as any good security guy would from general observation. But that was how he lived his life—with a divide between him and the people around him.

He juggled the two coffees in one hand while he unlocked the door, almost walking smack into Addison. "Leaving without me?"

"Oh, I thought you'd already left." She shook her head, her hand fluttering up to the pearls sitting along the neckline of her sleek emerald-green dress.

He swallowed past the lump that sat like a boulder in his throat. *Of course* she'd assumed he would walk out without saying goodbye. "Here, I got you a coffee."

"Thanks." They stood awkwardly in the middle of his apartment, neither one ready to make the first move.

In the light of day, they were unsure where things stood. Did she want to continue with the bet? Or had she changed her mind now that the lust-frenzied moment was over? Should he mention it or let it go?

Grow some balls, will you? It's like you've never spoken to a woman before.

He cleared his throat. "You look very nice."

To his surprise, a hearty chuckle bubbled out of her.

"Logan." She pressed a hand to his chest. "We don't have to pretend that we're dating. So cut the crap with the niceties, okay?"

"Fine. Is our bet still on?" He sipped his drink, silently giving himself a point for the faint blush that fanned out over her cheeks.

"I don't renege on a bet, no matter how unscrupulous my competitor."

"Then take off your panties."

She sucked on the inside of her cheek for a moment before placing her coffee and purse down on the table and reaching under her dress. Her hips wriggled as she dragged a scrap of lace down her thighs. He wasn't even sure a piece of material so small counted as underwear.

"Where do you want them?" She held them up with one finger, her direct expression daring him to balk.

"I don't care where you leave them, so long as they don't come to the office with you. I want to spend all day knowing there's nothing but a breeze under that pretty dress of yours."

"Your wish is my command." She dropped the thong onto the floor right where she stood. "Shall we go?"

She picked up her coffee and purse, shooting him a smug expression as she walked past him to the front door. "That bulge might be a bit of a problem in the office."

He didn't give her the satisfaction of looking down to what he already could feel was a rock-hard erection. "My bulge, my problem."

"Whatever you say, *Master*."

They walked to work in relative silence, but they didn't bother to enter the building separately. It wasn't unusual for them to arrive around the same time, so none of the staff members looked at them strangely. But Logan felt a prickle of unease under his skin. His life had been upended by Addison and her games.

And he was adding gas to the fire by bringing the teasing out into broad daylight.

"Good morning, Logan." His assistant, Emily, smiled up at him as he walked past.

Logan nodded briskly. The games could wait. He would not let his employees see that anything was going on between him and Addison.

"Rhys was here a moment ago looking for you. He said it had something to do with what you talked about yesterday," she said, cocking her eyebrow. "Very cryptic. Your calendar is clear until nine thirty if you want to catch him before your one-on-one with Owen. Rhys said he would be at the café downstairs."

Logan didn't even bother to check his emails before he turned tail and headed back the way he'd come. If there was an update on Addison's stalker, he wanted to know about it immediately.

As Emily had said, he found Rhys in the back corner table in the Brunswick Café, a regular haunt for Cobalt & Dane's employees.

"I hear you wanted to see me," Logan said, taking the seat across from Rhys. "I'm hoping you've got news."

"I do." Rhys sipped on a tall black coffee. "It might not be exactly what you want to hear, but we have some progress."

"Talk me through it." Logan leaned back in his chair. "In English, if possible."

Rhys smiled. "All right, boss, I'll dumb it down for you."

Logan grunted. "Watch it."

"So, after our chat yesterday we created a fake profile and email account for Addison and loaded it onto the dummy device. Then we enabled the virus by opening the attachment in the email. I had Quinn monitor the activity overnight, and yes—" he held up a hand "—before you ask, I told Quinn to not to talk about it. Despite the fact that I completely disagree with you keeping Addison in the dark."

"I appreciate that."

Rhys shook his head, but didn't argue. "The bad news is that our stalker figured out pretty quickly that it was a dummy account. We didn't have time to create fake content and files to keep him hunting around."

"Okay, so what *did* you find out?"

"Well, he's smart enough to use a proxy server to hide his location. So he might not be a tech genius, but he knows enough to cover his tracks, to some extent. However, we may have found something in the Trojan itself."

"Inside the virus?"

"Well, in the code. Quinn decompiled it so she could see if there was anything hidden inside that might point to the identity of either the hacker or, at the very least, to the person who wrote the code. Often these people will hide messages or signatures, kind of like how an artist might sign a painting."

"They're *not* artists," Logan said, his lip curling at thought of this guy plotting to harm Addison behind the safety of his computer screen.

"Well, they kind of are. Not all of this kind of code is bad. Sometimes it's used for penetration testing. We use a similar code to—"

Logan held up a hand. "Can we focus on the important stuff?"

"Right." Rhys nodded. "We found the name DaZettal in the code. I have no idea if this is our guy or just the person who made the Trojan, but it's something. I've got Quinn going through a few popular hacking forums to see if we can figure out who DaZettal is. As soon as I have more information, I'll let you know."

"Well done. I appreciate your work on this."

"Does this mean I'm back in the good books?" he asked drily.

A smile tugged at Logan's lips. Rhys had gotten himself in hot water a few months ago by sleeping with the employee of one of their clients. In some companies, it would have gotten him fired. But Logan knew loyalty when he saw it, and Rhys had the heart of a lion. Still, all Logan's employees were aware that if they crossed a line they'd be made to pay their penance.

And how are you paying your penance? What the hell would Daniel say if he knew what you'd done with Addison?

He swallowed his worries and pushed up from his chair. "Help me catch this fucker and then we'll talk."

10

ADDISON STOOD INSIDE the elevator, tapping her Louboutin heels impatiently while she watched the floor numbers count down. Her phone had rung twice during her last meeting and she knew it was the real estate agent calling about the office space.

With everything that'd happened last night, she'd forgotten to call the guy back. However, succumbing to a night of passion with Logan didn't mean her plans had changed. She *would* strike out on her own and she didn't want to do it working at her kitchen table or in a coffee shop. If people were going to take her seriously for once in her life, she needed to look the part. And that meant having a place of business.

Besides, she'd already decided to poach two of her staff members: one of her bright young recruits from the communications team and her HR manager. The three of them would make a fabulous team, and Addison couldn't do it all on her own. Hopefully they trusted her enough to make the leap from an established company to a start-up.

The elevator pinged as it arrived at the ground floor

and Addison quickly made her way through the foyer and out into the sunshine. The sun was high in the sky, the air starting to thicken with humidity. She found the missed call and dialed the number back.

"Hi, Richard, this is Addison. I'm sorry I didn't have the chance to call you back yesterday." She stood out of the way of the afternoon crowd, watching the city hustle and bustle right before her eyes.

"That's no problem at all," Richard said. "Is now a good time to talk?"

"Yes, absolutely."

Richard rattled off the details of the office space that was going to be available for viewing next week. Eight hundred square feet with one glass-walled office and room for a few desks in the main area. It shared a bathroom with one other business on the second floor. Close to the subway. Lots of natural light.

"It sounds perfect." Addison felt a flutter in her stomach. "It's exactly what I'm looking for."

"I can take you through it next Wednesday. The owner is in the process of clearing out his furniture as we speak."

"That's great." They arranged a time, and Addison put the meeting into her work calendar from her phone, being sure to mark it private so that Renee wouldn't be able to see it.

"What sort of business are you opening up?" Richard asked. "I have to double-check. The building owner is fairly conservative and has final say over all the tenants who move in, and I don't want anything to trip us up."

"It'll be a communications and corporate culture consulting company. We'll be helping small businesses manage their internal communications and staff development programs so they keep their best employees and attract the right candidates."

"Ah, okay." The *click-clack* of a computer keyboard sounded in the background. "I don't expect any issues with that."

"Perfect."

"The owner will also need to see your financials to make sure you can cover the first few months' rent. Do you have a statement you can send me?"

"I can get that information, but I'd prefer to look at the place before I hand any of my details over." She might not be a security expert, but she'd learned a thing or two, especially when it came to preventing identity theft and fraud.

"Sure, that's fine. I'll see you next week."

Addison ended the call and held her phone to her chest. This was really happening. Soon she'd be her own boss, a *real* boss. The idea of being totally independent thrilled her. Cobalt & Dane had been her whole working life to date, and while it would be hard to leave behind the company her father had started from nothing, she'd never feel like she'd be truly in charge of her own destiny until she did the same thing.

A breeze brushed along her legs, lifting the edge of her skirt. She suddenly remembered that she wasn't wearing any panties per Logan's order. Fisting the green fabric in one hand, she kept the dress pulled tight around her thighs. Guilt and excitement twisted in her stomach, wrapping around each other until she couldn't tell the two feelings apart.

Logan would be shocked to learn of her plans to leave. The company was everything to him, and he probably assumed it was everything to her, too. That shock could very well turn into anger when he found out that she planned on taking two staff members with her. He held loyalty in such high regard that he'd probably take the poaching personally.

It's not personal, it's business.

Leaving Cobalt & Dane was about her, not him. And she wouldn't be one of those women who feared chasing her dreams out of worry that people might not like her. If he took it as a personal attack, then that would be on him. She couldn't be held responsible for his feelings.

"What are you doing out here?" Logan's voice cut through the rush of traffic and people.

He walked toward her with Owen, the two men looking handsome as ever in their work outfits. They were quite the duo. Owen the ladies' man and Logan the heartbreaker.

No, he did not break your heart. He taught you a valuable lesson: that you shouldn't want relationships with men who have hero complexes.

"The office was getting a little stuffy," she replied, painting on a false smile. "I wanted some air."

"Good timing. We were coming back to collect you." Logan stopped in front of her, his closeness sending a thrill through her veins. "We're going to check out your apartment."

"Oh, goodie." Addison rolled her eyes.

"Don't argue." He leaned in closer. "Remember, you're mine for the next three days."

"How could I forget?" She tried to say it sarcastically but her body wasn't playing along. A warm flush spread up through her cheeks and she shifted on the spot.

"You're holding that dress pretty tight." He said with a glint in his eye. "Windy day?"

Part of her wanted to be annoyed at him for taking

advantage of his win. But if she'd come out victorious, she'd be using it against him all she could. They were two peas in a pod like that—competitive, fiercely so.

"Nothing I can't handle."

Owen raised a brow, barely stifling his smirk as he pretended not to notice the tension. It surprised her that Logan would flirt with her in front of Owen, but perhaps he was sending a message. Making sure his subordinate knew to keep his distance.

Ugh. She was no one's property.

"Owen, are you helping us out?" she asked, sending him a dazzling smile.

"You got it. We'll make sure your place is safe and sound." He raked a hand through his sandy hair.

"Excellent. I feel safer already."

She turned and walked back toward the building and Logan quickly caught up with her. "So you don't have a problem with Owen looking out for you, but when I do it I'm a monster?"

"More like a thorn in my side." Another breeze whooshed past and Addison kept her hands down by her sides, ready to hold her dress in place.

"What's the difference?"

"Owen would back off if I asked him to." She walked through the main doors to the Cobalt & Dane building. "You, on the other hand, are relentless and pushy."

"I happen to consider those two of my best qualities."

"And I'm sure one day you'll find a woman who appreciates an overbearing protector. But until that time, I'd appreciate some say in what goes on in my life."

THE WORDS HIT Logan square in the chest. Addison expected him to move on from her, to pursue other women as he'd done before. She assumed she wasn't the right woman for him. Or perhaps she thought they were incompatible on some basal level. And why should she think any differently? He'd said as much to her a few days ago and he'd given no indication that he'd changed his mind. But now, as he felt her slipping through his fingers, it made him want to hold on tighter...which was the very thing she was rallying against.

The thought bounced around in his head like a Ping-Pong ball. Of course he didn't want to lose her. She'd been part of his life since the moment she'd welcomed him into her home when his own family had abandoned him. She'd slipped her small teenage girl hand into his and dragged him through her front door. She'd squeezed an extra portion out of their meal for two and had given up her roast potatoes when he'd cleared his plate in record time. From day one, she'd made sure he knew he belonged.

But she was finally sick of his bullshit.

"I'll back off after my three days are up," he mumbled, raking a hand through his hair. "But right now, we need to check your apartment out."

"I know. And don't worry, I'm not going to ask you to change," she said. "I'm smart enough to realize you won't."

Owen caught up to them at the elevators and said something funny to Addison. The tinkling sound of her laugh was rattling around in Logan's head. He'd invited Owen along because he was trying to prove a point—that he wasn't threatened. That her safety came first.

But now he regretted that decision. They'd have to search through Addison's things to make sure that no one had managed to break in and bug her place. It felt wrong to have Owen do that, but if Logan changed his mind he'd have to face more questions—from both of them—that he wasn't ready to answer.

"I'm going to grab my things and I'll meet you out front in a few minutes, okay?" Addison didn't wait for a response and Logan watched the swish of her green dress as she walked away. Knowing there was nothing beneath the silk fabric was driving him insane.

"Is everything okay between you two?" Owen asked as they waited in the Cobalt & Dane reception area.

"Sure, why?"

Owen shrugged. "Sometimes I can't figure out if you want to kill each other or tear each other's clothes off."

In spite of himself, Logan let out a sharp laugh. "It's complicated."

"There's something more to this security issue, isn't there?"

Logan glanced around the space, making sure there were no prying eyes or sneaky ears in the immediate vicinity. "Yeah, there is. We didn't want to worry the team, but we have reason to believe that Addison has a stalker, and he's tampered with her apartment."

"Shit." Owen shook his head. "I'm happy to help out in any way I can."

"Good. The first thing you can do is keep that information to yourself."

"Done."

By the time they made it to Addison's apartment, she was jumpy as all hell. He tried to ease her nerves by joking around, but she was having none of it. The three of them rode the elevator up to her apartment in awkward silence. A crease had formed between her brows as she stared at the numbers climbing up on the small screen. No wonder Owen couldn't work out whether they wanted to kill each other or tear each other's clothes off—they had this crazy push and pull of attraction that made even Logan's head spin.

What was he supposed to do? This was a very real threat to her safety. Perhaps it was unwise to withhold the information about the second email from her. But he'd tell her about it once Rhys had more information. She was stressed enough as it was, and telling her that they'd found a hacker's pseudonym wouldn't put her mind at ease.

The elevator dinged and they filed out into the hallway. When Addison stopped at her front door, keys in hand, Logan spotted something on the floor.

"Wait," he said as he bent down to scoop it up. A white envelope had been partially slipped under the door. No name or any other identifying information was on the paper.

"Don't say you're going to start opening my mail, too?" Addison held her hand out.

"Of course not, but open it slowly. We don't know what's inside." He felt over the envelope before giving it up. There didn't appear to be anything inside except for paper.

She slipped her thumb under the seal and opened it. Blood rushed in Logan's ears as she pulled a single sheet of paper out. It could be anything—a notice from building management, a request from a neighbor. But his gut told him it was something far more sinister than that.

He resisted the urge to take the paper from her as her face paled. "What does it say?"

"An eye for an eye." Her voice was small, shaky. "It says that Dad took something from them and now they're going to take something from me."

"They?"

"There's no name or signature." She drew a breath and turned the note around so they could read it. Basic white paper, Times New Roman font. Nothing that could possibly tell them a goddamn thing about the sender.

"We'll figure this out," Owen said, placing a hand on her shoulder. "You've got the best security company in the world at your disposal."

"That's very reassuring." She tried to smile but it didn't quite reach her eyes.

"Come on, let's do the inspection." Logan nodded toward the door. "I'll talk to building management when we're done and check out the camera footage again."

Addison unlocked her front door and they entered her apartment. Sunlight streamed in from the windows that ran the length of the main room, the light bouncing off her pristine white furniture. It was hard to believe anything sinister would happen in a space that looked more like a magazine spread than a home.

"Owen, you examine the front door and see if the lock has been tampered with, while Addison and I start from the back rooms. We'll meet in the middle."

"Sure thing." Owen got to work and Logan motioned for Addison to follow him.

"What are we looking for?" Her hands knotted in front of her.

"Any signs of tampering with the locks on your doors or windows. It's unlikely anyone would be able to get in via the balcony, since we're quite high up. But I've seen stranger things. Then we'll check for monitoring or surveillance devices." He paused outside her bedroom door. "Rhys also gave me a program to install on your laptop which will run a scan for any viruses and give him access to monitor your device until we figure out what's going on."

"What do you mean he's going to monitor my personal computer?" Her eyes narrowed. "Didn't either of you think to consult me on this?"

"If this person tried to contact you through your work email—where there's likely to be some high-grade security—it stands to reason he might have tried your personal computer, too. We've talked about this."

"But I haven't received any strange emails on my personal computer."

"It's no big deal, Addi. We won't be reading your diary or anything."

She gritted her teeth. "You don't get it. How can you agree to these things on my behalf without consulting me first?"

"Because I'm doing my job, like I would with any other client."

"I am *not* your client." Her dark eyes flashed.

"The only reason you would be so pissed about this—especially after the note left on your doorstep—was if you were worried about us finding something on your computer." He leaned against the door frame at the entrance of her bedroom, the uneasy feeling returning. Addison treasured her independence, sure, but she also understood what evil they faced in the world. There was only one reason she'd be getting *this* upset about a routine computer scan. "What are you hiding?"

"Nothing." Her face was pale, drawn. "Is it so inconceivable that I want my private life kept private?"

In Logan's experience, the people who were overly concerned with privacy were the ones who had skeletons in their closets. "It's not inconceivable, but your privacy is the lesser concern right now."

"Fine. I'll fire the laptop up while you do whatever—" she waved her hand in the air "—you need to do. Then we can go to the store and buy a baby monitor so you can keep an eye on me overnight."

He sighed as she walked off, her heels loud in the quiet apartment. Something was up with Addison; the certainty of it dug deep in his gut. She'd always battled with her overprotective father for her independence—and then against him more recently. But this time there was a real and ongoing threat to her safety. And yet she refused to accept it, which combined with what she'd said at the cottage made him suspicious. She might not like the way he went about things, but he would get to the bottom of this mystery—both who was after her and what she was hiding.

11

ADDISON'S HEART AND head pounded in unison. If Rhys got access to her computer, all the documents she'd been working on—business plans, budget spreadsheets and research—would be at his fingertips. And if she knew anything for certain, it was that Rhys's loyalty lay with Logan.

She couldn't have either of them finding out her plans until she was ready to put them into action. Until everything was set up so they couldn't talk her out of it.

Addison found her laptop sitting on the pristine white coffee table. She dropped down onto the couch in preparation for damage control. The best she could do was hide the files and hope that they would simply monitor the computer rather than snoop around on it.

She made her planning folder invisible and dragged all the relevant emails from her inbox into a folder called "Online Shopping." No man would venture there, surely. It wasn't perfect, but it would have to do.

A few moments later, Logan reappeared. "Hey, is the laptop all booted up?"

"Yeah. It's all yours." She pushed it toward him and leaned back into the couch. "Will it take long?"

"No, it should only take a few minutes. Why? You got somewhere else to be?" He said it in a way that diverted her attention from all the security drama and funneled it into the dirty section of her imagination.

Why did he have to be so goddamn addictive? She couldn't seem to go an hour without thinking about how much she wanted him. Even with all his annoying habits.

"Maybe," she said cryptically.

"Have you forgotten our deal?" He'd plugged a USB into her laptop and was installing Rhys's program as though they weren't talking about a sex game within earshot of their employee.

"No, I have not."

"So you're reneging" He didn't look up.

"I don't renege"

"Good. Because we've got plans tonight."

She rolled her eyes. "Want to clue me in on what they might be?"

"We're going to find out what 'an eye for an eye' means."

"I know what it means."

"Not in this context. Unless you're keeping something from me?" He glanced up from the laptop. "Are you?"

"Of course not," she huffed. "Besides, you know everything about my life so I doubt something that big would have slipped past your eagle eyes."

"We'll talk about my eagle eyes later," Logan said under his breath as Owen approached them.

"I've checked out the door. There doesn't appear to be any tampering of the locks." Owen paused, his brow furrowed. "One of the neighbors came past. I talked to him but he hasn't seen anything unusual of late. He didn't know anything about a letter being dropped off, said most mail goes straight into the boxes downstairs."

"That's right." Addison nodded. "Which means this creep has been snooping around again."

"I called building management and asked them to keep an eye out for anyone trying to sneak past." Logan rubbed at the back of his neck. "There's someone at the concierge desk twenty-four/seven, right?"

"Yeah. If a strange man came past, the concierge should have stopped him." She drummed her fingers on her leg. "All guests are supposed to sign in but he did manage to slip past last time, so it could have happened again."

"Are there any people who don't have to sign in?"

"The guys who deliver takeout to the building. The concierge buzzes them in and they go straight up to the floor." She knew for a fact that they often breezed right through the foyer of the building without attracting much attention. It would be the perfect cover.

"Okay, good. That'll give us something to look for on the surveillance footage." Logan bobbed his head. "From my search, it doesn't seem as if the guy has done anything here other than the delivery of the note. So I think that and the security cameras should be our area of focus."

"What else can I do to help?" Owen asked. For the guy who was always laughing and joking, his face was uncharacteristically serious.

"Head back to the office and update Rhys, but keep it quiet. We're only telling those who need to know—no sense in worrying the troops."

Owen nodded. "Good call."

"My full focus is on figuring out what this guy wants and ensuring that Addison is kept out of harm's way," Logan said. "So I have to ask you to step up and take care of the day-to-day stuff, okay?"

"Consider it done." Owen raked a hand through his shaggy blond hair. "If there are any problems, I'll check in."

"Good. We'll touch base on Monday morning."

Addison stayed on the couch as Owen left. She'd kicked off her heels and tucked her feet up underneath her. Her life was feeling further and further out of her control by the minute.

"I don't understand what this guy wants," she said. "An eye for an eye? What did Dad do that was so bad?"

"He put the bad guys away for a living. Think about how many people might have been sent to jail because of evidence he gathered in the course of his career." He shrugged. "I know for a fact that he received threats on a few occasions."

He'd never told her that. Neither of them had. It was simply one more thing they'd shared that she hadn't. One more thing she wasn't allowed to be part of because she needed to be "protected." She swallowed against the bitter taste in her mouth.

"It comes with the territory, unfortunately," Logan continued. "You go up against dangerous people and they bite back."

"But why now? Dad's been gone for two years and he was out of the action for a good twelve months before that because of the cancer." A lump lodged itself in her throat, but she jammed the emotions down. He would want her to focus now, not grieve. "Why would someone come after me out of the blue for something my dad might have done more than three years ago? It doesn't make sense."

"There has to be something we're missing. A catalyst."

She rolled her eyes. "Obviously."

"You being so testy about everything doesn't help the situation." He frowned at her. "I know this is an imposition and I'm sure you'd love to kick my ass out of here—"

"I would."

"But that doesn't change the fact that there is someone after you who's most likely unhinged and who has already proved to be dangerous. Addi, I don't care if this makes you hate me. I've fucked up too many times in my life to let your annoyance get in the way of doing what's right." He sighed. "Your dad was the only thing that kept me from ending up in jail after my mom died. I don't take my promise to him lightly."

She tilted her head, intrigued in spite of her bad mood. He'd never talked much about how he came to work for her father. "Why do you think you would have ended up in jail?"

"I was on a bad path back then."

"After you left the army?"

"After I got kicked out, you mean."

It didn't surprise her; his stubbornness wouldn't suit military life. But he'd never admitted it before. "Why were you kicked out?"

"I went AWOL. When I found out my mom had died I just…" His Adam's apple bobbed. "I didn't know what to do. I couldn't handle being on base, I couldn't handle my commander screaming at me. I took off, like a coward."

"You were young." She reached out to him, her fingers curling over his hand. "That was enough for them to kick you out?"

"Yeah, because I was gone longer than forty days and the commander had it in for me from the start. That was all he needed to give me an administrative discharge. He could have disciplined me, but he said I had 'no viable future' with them. That I wasn't fit to be in the army." Logan's eyes were fixed on something in the distance, as though the answers to his personal turmoil were located high in the late-afternoon skyline. "He said that no good would come of a messed-up kid like me."

"That's awful." Her chest clenched as though her body were trying to absorb his pain. "Why did you take so long to go back?"

"I had only intended to stay for the funeral, but..." His face became marble-hard. "I found out my dad had already shacked up with another woman. His wife's body wasn't even in the ground yet and he was already fucking someone else. And he'd invited her into our home. They were there when I arrived."

Oh God. She couldn't even begin to imagine what that must have been like. Her own father had never even looked at another woman after her mom passed. He'd been as devoted to her as a widower as he'd been as a husband.

"I lost it, just about smashed every plate in the house. He's still with that same woman now, so you can see why I'm not too welcome at family gatherings." He shook his head and let out a bitter laugh. "A friend referred me to your dad, said he had a security gig and was looking for muscle. When I started working for him, it was the first time I felt like I might have a future after all."

There wasn't an ounce of emotion in his rigid expression, but Addison knew that was a sign of a storm raging inside him. He'd tempered himself over the years, learning to react internally first. To use his poker face as protection. To hide the anger and sadness that had been brewing in him for years.

But she knew where to look for the truth.

"He cared about you a lot," she said, moving closer to him on the couch and leaning her shoulder on his shoulder. "You were the son he never had. I was so jealous when you came along."

His head snapped in her direction, his dark eyes burning intently into hers. "Why on earth would you have been jealous of me? You were his pride and joy."

"Because you shared things with him that I couldn't. You talked shop, you chased the bad guys together, and I had to sit at home like some delicate little bubble girl." The catch her voice belied her calm tone. "You did all the things that I could never do. You had a place by his side because he *wanted* you there."

"Addi." The tension around his eyes softened. "He wanted you by his side. Why do you think he brought you into the business? He was so proud of you."

"Not enough to let me do the *real* work," she said bitterly. "I wanted so bad to be in the security side of things, but I let him talk me into business school. I thought it was because he valued my skills in those areas but I'm not so sure about that now."

"You believe he manipulated you?"

"It sounds so bad when you say it like that…but, yeah." She swallowed. On the surface she should have been mad at her father, but she couldn't bring herself to give in to resentment. He'd done what he could to raise her right—being a single father couldn't have been easy.

He'd had to play both mother and father to her, doing everything from helping her with her homework to braiding her hair to wading through the atrocities of puberty. And never once had he complained.

"Did you really want to work on the security stuff, or was it about being closer to him?" Logan asked.

The question stalled her. Logan was right; it wasn't that she was particularly passionate about security. It was something much deeper than that. "I wanted to be equal. I wanted to be *respected* instead of being the paperwork girl."

"You know, he told me once that you joining him at the company was the proudest moment of his life."

The words hit her like a freight train to the solar plexus. "What?"

"Remember that day we switched over the payroll system and we almost wiped out all the employee data?"

She groaned. "God, do I ever. I thought we were going to have to key it all in manually and that we'd miss the deadline to pay everyone that month."

"Your dad said to me that if it wasn't for you managing those areas of the business, that he would never have been able to expand the company the way he did. *You* were the reason we could grow, because you kept the lights on when things got bad. You made sure that our bills got paid, that we always had an office space, that we kept track of our money."

"Just doing my job." She tried to make light of his words, but the truth was she could barely breathe. Of course she knew her father loved her, but he was a tough man. One who'd never spoken his emotions aloud.

"No, Addi. You're the heart and soul of Cobalt & Dane. You're the only person who could fill your father's shoes and…" He raked a hand through his hair, suddenly looking like that boy she'd fallen for all those years ago. "Thanks for not walking out on me after what I did."

Guilt trickled like poison through her veins. Never once had he acknowledged that she'd stuck by him—in a business sense—even after the personal stuff had gotten messy, much less thanked her for it. Why did he have to start being a good guy now?

"My pleasure," she whispered.

ADDISON DIDN'T MAKE eye contact, her hands toying with the hem of her dress. He would have seen less confusion on her face if he'd announced aliens were about to land on the planet.

This is why you don't do the touchy-feely stuff. You can't even give her a compliment without fucking it up.

"Anyway." He paused to clear his throat. "We should probably go through some of the old case files."

"You think we'll find something there?"

"It's a place to start. The security footage is probably not going to give us any more than it did before, so we have to get creative. The note *has* to mean something."

"Why would he leave a note if it could possibly give us a clue as to his identity?"

"Maybe he's getting frustrated at his lack of progress. Or maybe he wants to toy with you. Guys who do these kinds of things can get cocky, thinking they hold all the power."

"Right." She nodded. "Well, let me get changed. I don't want to be digging through files in this dress."

She was still so close to him on the couch. So close that he wanted to bundle her up in his arms and keep her safe and warm and close to him, where she belonged.

She doesn't belong to you, idiot. You blew that chance.

He watched as she stood, her long, lean limbs so graceful in movement. Like a dancer. What he'd give to wake up to that body every morning. To that smile. To those loving hands and lips and eyes.

"Addi?" He reached for her hand.

"Yeah?"

"I swear on my mother's grave that we're going to find this guy. I will take personal pride in nailing him to a wall for you."

A smile quirked on her lips. "That's the most romantic thing anyone has ever said to me."

"I guess I'll have to try harder then."

Her rich brown eyes didn't reveal anything. She was too careful for that.

HALF AN HOUR later Logan and Addison walked into Cobalt & Dane's archive room. It was on a different floor from their main offices. The dusty little room was full of cardboard boxes and needed to be dragged into the current decade.

"Aren't you glad I forced everyone to come through and label all these boxes correctly?" Addison tossed a smug smile over her shoulder as they walked through the door. "At least now we'll know what we're looking at."

He was grateful for her system, but he wasn't about to admit it to her. "I bet you have dirty dreams about organizing things. Just you and some hot stud with a calculator."

She snorted. "And what do you dream about? Having a girl on her knees while she submits to you in every possible way? Oh, wait. That's probably true"

Damn right it was. The thought of getting Addison

down on her knees made his cock stir. He'd love to bind those delicate wrists and bend her over the rickety little table in here.

He cleared his throat. "You said it, not me. And don't be putting ideas in my head. We've got work to do."

When he'd seen the outfit Addison had changed into back at her apartment—her gorgeous body poured into a pair of tiny denim shorts and a tight white tank top—he'd wanted to throw her onto the couch. They'd acted like the conversation about their families, about their regrets, had never happened. Because that's what he did. Avoiding emotion was the only way to go, because a bleeding heart had never served him in life. He had to be careful around Addison because she had a way of making him open up like a tap.

"Where do we even start?" She threw her hands up in the air.

The room was lined with metal shelves containing box after box of files. Not all of them were case files, though, they had boxes of records to keep for tax purposes. Old employee files, training documents. The list went on.

Thanks to Addison, the different types of files had been sorted into areas and labeled. Case files were marked with a big red *C* in the top right-hand corner of the box, followed by the month and year the case was closed. Cases that hadn't been closed were marked with a *U* for unresolved.

"My guess is that we can leave the unresolved cases for now," Logan said, placing his laptop onto the table in the center of the room. "We've got the basic records in the case management system, so let's look for cases that resulted in a handoff to police and go from there."

She nodded. "That seems like a logical approach."

"I do come up with *some* good ideas," he teased as he pulled up their case management database.

It wasn't a fancy one like some of the bigger companies might use, but it allowed them to keep track of the important information for each case—like the date Cobalt & Dane was engaged, which consultants worked on the job, the initial request, the date the case was closed and a brief description of the outcome. Each case was assigned a type to indicate whether it was an ongoing or onetime service, and the outcomes were sorted to allow them to analyze how the company was most commonly being utilized. The entire system had been Addison's design, her knack for information and organization making their lives easier in situations like this.

"Okay, so we'll narrow the search to find only closed cases." He clicked the appropriate checkbox and Addison hovered over his shoulder. The end of her long ponytail tickled his shoulder and he tried not to be distracted by the scent of her perfume. "Let's cut the date off around the time your father stopped working. We'll keep it open from the very beginning, although I think some of the earlier cases don't have much information."

"No, Dad had the same approach to paperwork as you do."

He ignored the dig. "We'll look only at cases that resulted in a handoff to police." He stared at the screen warily, knowing how many cases would *still* show up in the search. "Let's filter it also by cases that were assigned to your dad."

"This seems like a lot of guesswork."

"There's a good deal of guesswork in what we do.

Besides, if this thing spits out ten thousand records, is that going to get us anywhere?"

"No," she admitted. "But filtering out the right records won't help us, either. It's like a wild-goose chase."

But sitting around worrying would also be futile. Logan was still waiting to hear from Rhys if he'd uncovered any further information on the person who'd created the Trojan. He made a mental note to call Rhys once Addison was distracted with the case files.

He clicked the search button on the computer system and the screen filled up with prospective cases for them to look at. "Okay, now we start searching. Let's work from the most current cases and go backward."

Addison stared forlornly at the boxes lining the walls. "This is going to take forever."

He read out the dates from the first few files and they pulled the corresponding boxes. Dust plumed as they tossed the lids onto the floor. Each box was filled with slim folders labeled with case numbers. The plan had always been to digitize the old files, since they'd now moved to a paperless system, but no one had gotten around to it.

"What exactly should I be looking for?" she asked.

For once, she was seeking out his advice. Small step though it might be, the fact that he could help her with something pleased him.

"The sheet on top of the file should have a summary of the case. Look for anything that references a conviction or punitive measure. Something bad enough that might cause a crooked guy to seek revenge."

"I hope we find the guy in these more recent files," she said. "We haven't been doing the summary sheets for all that long. Dad thought they were a waste of time when I first suggested them."

"Stubborn men can be resistant to change."

"You talking about yourself or about him?" She tip-toed her fingers through the files in the box until she found what she was looking for. "You seemed to think it was wasted effort as well, if my memory serves me correctly."

"Sounds like something I would say." He pulled a file from his own box and leafed through the information inside. Nothing.

"I still haven't managed to figure out if you're difficult on purpose or if it's just something that comes naturally." A smile quirked on her lips.

"Me, difficult? Never." He pulled another file. "Now, you on the other hand…"

"Only someone who has as strong a personality as I do would be able to put up with having *you* as a business partner. So really, our stubbornness makes us well matched. Two perfectly difficult peas in a pod."

"Whatever you say, Addi."

Her fingers tucked a loose strand of blond hair behind her ear as she leaned over the file box. Tension formed a crease between her brows. "We're going to figure this out, aren't we? I mean, you do these kinds of things all the time and you always find the bad guys, right?"

The tightness in her voice blew a hole in his chest. Strong as she was, even Addison could be worn down by the fear of someone watching. Waiting. Hoping for a moment to strike.

"Of course we will. Trust me, there's nothing I won't do to take care of you," he said. An odd feeling clutched at his chest, squeezing the air out of his lungs.

On any other case, he'd be cool as a cucumber. But this was different. He *had* to figure out who was after her, because his gut told him that the creep wouldn't stop at vague notes and computer viruses. He wanted to harm Addison, and Logan wouldn't let that happen.

12

A FEW HOURS later Addison leaned back against the shelves and rubbed at her foot, which had fallen asleep. The pile of cases requiring further review had grown as they'd worked, though far fewer ended in some kind of police involvement than Addison had initially surmised.

"This could be something," she said, tapping the open folder in her lap. "It's a case from five years ago. A maintenance manager in a co-op building was breaking into apartments while the tenants were on vacation."

"You'd be surprised how often that kind of thing happens," Logan said. "What was the outcome?"

"The notes say he ended up getting a felony conviction for aggravated robbery even though the defense argued that no one was in the apartment at the time of the burglary. I guess they must have had some proof he carried a weapon even if there was no intent to use it."

"A harsh sentence could certainly make for an enemy, especially if he feels like the charges were inflated."

Addison nodded. "But wouldn't he still be in jail if he got that kind of a conviction?"

"What's his name? We'll look him up." Logan pushed

up from the floor, taking a moment to stretch his arms above his head.

She tried not to look as his T-shirt revealed a sliver of taut skin at his belly. The cotton stretched across his chest, revealing the outline of muscles she knew felt like heaven under her palms. It would be wonderful to forget all about her stalker and her secret and indulge in a little pleasure.

When did her life get so damn complicated?

Addison forced her eyes back down to the file. "Uh, his name is Adrian Marco Vendetti. Born 1955, Brownsville, New York."

Logan leaned over the small square table where his laptop sat and typed the name into a search engine. A few moments later he let out a surprised *hmm*.

"He's dead."

Addison blinked and rose to join him. "Huh?"

"He was killed during a prison riot, it seems. According to this article, Vendetti's son is suing the state for wrongful death." Logan paused while Addison leaned over him to see the article. "Vendetti had been denied a transfer after a fight with the guy who ended up killing him."

"Brutal."

He scrolled further down the page. "His son is the one pursuing the legal action." He cocked his head. "Michael Zetta. Why does that name sound familiar?"

"No idea." Addison shook her head. "It doesn't sound familiar to me."

At that moment her stomach grumbled loud enough to startle them both. Logan chuckled. "I guess we should take a dinner break."

She glanced down at her watch. It was 9:00 p.m.

"Why don't we call it a night? We'll take the files back to my place and keep working on them over the weekend."

"Is that your way of saying you'd like me to hang around?" He closed the laptop and turned to her.

"I've accepted the inevitable. You're not going anywhere, so I may as well embrace it." For some reason the words comforted rather than stifled her.

In the past week, Logan had been by her side more than ever. They'd rekindled the spark that had drawn them to each other over the years, the spark that she'd thought had been extinguished when she'd turned up at his door to find him with another woman.

Just because he cares about you doesn't mean he knows how to treat you right. Don't get attached. Don't be vulnerable again unless you're prepared to get hurt.

"Well, it's not a glowing invitation, but I'll take it." He offered her a roguish grin. "You're a hard woman to please, Addison Cobalt."

"Yeah, right," she scoffed. "You're insufferable. I'm sure other guys wouldn't find me hard to please."

"And you think another guy could rev you up the way I do?" He folded his arms across his chest, the muscles bulging under the cotton of his T-shirt. Clearly, her words had hit their mark. "Would another guy have been able to convince you to go to work without panties? I bet you didn't even put them back on when you got changed."

Heat flared through her, pooling in her cheeks. And between her legs. "What makes you say that?"

"Because you like the thrill of being bossed around."

Oh, how she wanted to slap the smug expression off his face with one of the case files. "Bullshit."

Hate it as she might, there was no denying the denim shorts did brush deliciously against her bare sex. She ached for him. Against her will, her body craved his like a drug. And he was right; the power play between them only served to build excitement in her until it felt as if a tornado were blowing through her body. No other man had ever come close to making her feel the way he did.

Don't let him suck you in.

"Prove it," he challenged. "Take your shorts off now and show me you put your panties back on."

"No way." Her eyes darted around the room. "There are cameras in here."

"Cameras that *we* own." He shrugged. "That's the best thing about being the boss—no one can punish you. We can do whatever we like."

"This is…ridiculous."

Dammit, why did he have to be so right about her? He knew her better than anyone, and right now he was totally using it to his advantage.

"What's ridiculous is you maintaining this charade." His smile morphed from amused to wolfish. His dark eyes practically glittered with excitement. "I'm in your head, Addi. And you love it."

He took a step toward her and she immediately backed up. "You've got an inflated sense of your abilities, Dane."

"Oh I'm *Dane* now, am I? What's the matter, baby? Too afraid to say my name in case your shorts melt right off your body?"

"You're *so* full of it." She rolled her eyes, but as her back hit the shelves she realized she was in trouble. "So goddamn full of it."

"I think the lady doth protest too much." He stalked over to her, his hands landing on her waist. His thumbs brushed the waistband of her shorts, pushing up her tank top. "It's okay. I'm more than happy to conduct an independent investigation."

He lowered to his knees in front of her, his warm breath tickling her bare skin. A ripple of awareness shot through her, like he'd found a secret *on* switch to her entire nervous system. Everything was heightened—the sensitivity of her skin, the feel of his palms running over her hips. He electrified her. Burned her from the inside out.

But that was the thing about flames—the warmth was great until you got too close.

"Let's see what you've been hiding under here." He toyed with the button on her shorts for a moment before popping it loose. "Are you as immune to me as you say?"

The moment he grabbed the zipper and dragged it down, the fight left Addison's body. He had her. Cornered. Trapped.

Totally and utterly at his mercy.

"Just as I thought." He dragged the denim shorts down her thighs until they pooled around her ankles. "You're a good girl at heart, Addi. Good at following orders. Good at giving me what I want."

"Screw you," she bit out, ready to push him away.

But the moment his lips pressed against her sex, she was lost. His tongue pushed between her folds, seeking out her clit. Not a moment was wasted. "Oh, you will. You'll be so ready to screw me that I won't even have time to get you back to your apartment. You're already so wet for me."

A cry caught in her throat as he sucked at her. He extracted one foot from the shorts tangled around her ankles and threw her leg over his shoulder, and she melted. His fingers dug into her ass, supporting her. Holding her steady while he feasted. It was the kind of reckless abandon that she never allowed herself in life. The kind that came with an inherent sense of risk.

But it didn't matter now. Nothing mattered except the orgasm that welled deep inside her.

"I can feel you shaking," he murmured against her. "It's so good, Addi. So fucking good."

"No kidding," she gasped, her hands threading through his hair as a tremor ripped through her. "Oh, Logan."

"That's it, Addi. Let it all out."

Her head lolled back against the case files as she struggled to stay upright. Waves of pleasure lapped at her. Her hips rolled in time with the sensation, her body seeming to move of its own accord.

"I'm close," she gasped.

"Not yet." He pulled away, ignoring her cry of protest. "I want to be inside you when you come."

Fishing the wallet out of his pants, he located one of the condoms he kept stashed there. In seconds, he'd stripped his pants and sheathed himself. His body seemed to vibrate.

"Come here." She reached for him and they landed hard against the shelving unit.

"God, Addi." He tugged her leg over his hip, guiding his cock to her entrance with his hand. "I need you so bad."

"I need you, too." She gasped as he pushed inside her.

The feeling of him breaching her tight sex was near divine. His warm skin and greedy hands overwhelmed her senses as he thrust into her. Hard. Desperate. This wouldn't be delicate. It wouldn't be sweet or even sensual. Whenever they came together, there was a rawness that undid her.

"Take me," she gasped.

He hoisted her up and she wrapped both legs around him, her thighs squeezing his waist. The metal shelving unit groaned as they writhed. She reached up with one hand and wrapped her fingers around the edge of a shelf, trying to find leverage to meet his thrusts.

"You ruin me." He buried his face into the crook of her neck. "This feels too fucking good."

His hands were all over her, as though he had to touch every inch of her in order to survive. Her body trembled as she lost herself. Eyes clamped shut, she let the feeling take her over. Lights danced behind her lids and she was vaguely aware of his name falling from her lips.

As she tried to push the post-orgasm fog from her mind, she felt his strong hands lower her to the ground. Being in his arms shouldn't have felt like the best place in the world. Being at his mercy shouldn't have felt like everything she'd ever wanted.

But it did. And now she was at risk of giving herself completely over to him.

As ADDISON'S BREATH SLOWED, she stirred against Logan's chest. How long they'd been standing there wrapped up in each other, he had no idea. But he wasn't about to move until she was ready. Truth be told, he would have stood in that same position until he lost all sensation in his arms just to have her curled up against him.

"I'm starving," she mumbled, her face rubbing against the base of his neck. "Need pizza now."

They grabbed the files and swung past their regular pizza joint on the way back to his apartment. It struck him how at ease he was with Addison—how well he knew her favorite pizza toppings, the jokes that would make her laugh, that she was superstitious about not stepping on a crack in the street.

She'd pulled away from him in the last two years and he'd studiously ignored how much he missed her. How his life had a giant gaping hole in it.

And now, even though she'd come back to him, there was a sense of panic that wouldn't budge. A foreboding hanging over his head like a thundercloud. He was at risk of losing her again, but he didn't know why.

"I regret the way we ended things last time," he blurted out.

They walked into his apartment and Addison raised a brow as she put their dinner onto the coffee table. "What?"

"Last time." He cleared his throat as he lowered the box of files to the floor. "After we, you know…"

Someone take me out to a pasture and shoot me. It'll be less painful.

"Since when are you the blushing wallflower?" She laughed, but her eyes avoided his. It was easy to see that hurt still lay there. She hadn't forgotten what he'd done.

"It was a dick thing to do."

She shrugged. "You don't owe me anything."

"I owe you my respect." He raked a hand through his hair, grappling for the right thing to say. If only he could better express himself. Unfortunately, years of keeping his distance from others made it hard for him to open up. "And, uh, jumping into bed with someone else right away wasn't very respectful."

"Why did you do it?" She folded her arms across her chest, creating a shield between them.

Why, indeed? Because he was stupid to epic proportions.

"I was terrified of losing someone else." First his mother, then his father, then Daniel...he seemed to lose people quicker than he could build relationships.

"So you made sure you *would* lose me. That doesn't make a whole lot of sense."

"No, it doesn't. But I guess my screwed-up brain figured that I couldn't technically lose you if I didn't have you in the first place." It sounded even dumber aloud than it had in his head. "And I felt like I'd pissed on your father's memory by being with you in that way."

"You think he'd prefer for you to treat me like a piece of trash?" Her voice trembled. "I'm not disposable, Logan."

This wasn't going the way he wanted it to. It was clear Addison still didn't trust him, and why should she?

"I'm sorry." She held up a hand, her mask clicking back into place. "I shouldn't have said that. It was out of line."

He swallowed. "I deserve it."

"No, you don't. You're only human and so am I." She sucked in a deep breath. "I have high expectations and sometimes that makes me go a little crazy. We weren't in a relationship, so I had no claim on you."

This was the out he'd hoped for all those months ago. The acknowledgment that technically he hadn't done the wrong thing. But technicalities were worth shit and *nothing* would make him feel better about hurting her.

"Still, I shouldn't have rubbed it in your face like that."

"True, but the past is the past. Right?" She smiled brightly. Fake. "Let's not talk about this ever again and I promise I'll try to forget it happened."

It should have been what he wanted, but her suggestion turned like sour milk in his stomach. He didn't want her to forget. He wanted her to remember his hands tangling in her hair, his teeth marking her skin. He wanted her to be consumed by the memories of the fire they'd made together, just as he was.

He wanted her to be his.

"Sure." He shook his head, the thoughts bouncing like Ping-Pong balls against the inside of his skull.

What do you mean you want her to be yours? So you can inflict your fucked-up issues on her? No way, no how. Not ever.

"We should eat," she said, opening up the pizza box to grab a slice. "You don't want to see me when I'm hangry."

"Nothing you could possibly do would scare me. I've seen a lot, trust me." He dropped down beside her and patted her knee as if nothing was wrong.

But his feelings for Addison had deepened. They'd gone from an insistent whisper to a roar that had the force of a buffalo stampede. How much longer would he be able to pretend that casual sex would satisfy him? Fulfill him?

But you can't give her what she deserves.

Couldn't he? For Addison, maybe he could be the upstanding guy who communicated and compromised and trusted. For her, maybe he could change. If she didn't leave him first.

13

BY THE TIME Monday rolled around, Logan and Addison had barely left his apartment. Between the white-hot sex and the old case files, she'd been unable to concentrate on anything else. On any*one* else.

They'd cooked dinner together last night and let it burn in the saucepan while they lost themselves in pleasure on the dining table.

"You'd better hope I can get that horrible burned smell out of this place," she said as she turned the coffee machine on. "You're such a distraction."

"Me?" He pressed a hand to his chest in mock outrage. "You were the one who decided it would be a good idea to cook naked."

A sly smile lifted at the corner of her lips. "I had an apron on."

"Yes, and that glorious ass of yours was hanging out. What was I supposed to do?" He growled the question into her ear as he pressed her against the kitchen counter. His hands were everywhere—cupping her face, kneading her backside, parting her thighs so he could stroke her still-needy sex.

"You're like a drug. You know that, right?" She sank her teeth down into her lip as he rubbed his stubble-coated jaw along her neck. "Potent. Intoxicating. Addictive."

"Addictive?" He nipped at her. "And here I was thinking it was time to up the dosage."

Her head lolled back. "I don't know how much more I can take."

Like any good drug, Logan made her forget the potential side effects. The risks. She'd sink into his pleasure-filled fog without a worry about her heart. Without a worry about what would happen when reality came crashing down on them. He'd get bored, find another woman. Leave her in pieces.

He said he regrets what happened. Maybe he won't *hurt you again.*

Still, there was the slight matter of her plans to start her own business. Even if Logan had dealt with his commitment issues, Addison still needed to be her own boss. To do something that made her feel worthwhile. How could she indulge in fantasies about living happily ever after when she was planning to break away from him?

"You're a lot hardier than you think," he said. "You've taken a lot of knocks over the years and you're still here, still fighting."

"I am, aren't I?" She turned her face to his and captured his lips with her own.

A tremor ran through her as he slid his tongue along hers. God, he tasted so good. Earthy. Male. Like sex and sin and home all rolled into one.

His hands snaked up her back, crushing her to him. He was hard again, ready. Always ready.

"Logan," she groaned. "We have to go to work."

"Do we?" A wicked grin pulled at his lips. "Why don't we play hooky?"

"We can't."

"I'll give you a permission slip." His teeth scraped down her neck and he filled his palm with her breast. "Valid for one day of mind-blowing sex and as many orgasms as you can handle."

"But what about the case files?"

He stilled and she could practically hear the cogs turning in his brain. "You're right."

Over the weekend, it'd been easy to pretend that her stalker was nothing but a figment of her imagination. She and Logan had created their own perfect bubble, impenetrable to the outside world. Complete with locked doors and her own personal bodyguard. With him, she was safe and secure. Wanted.

But that could all be blown apart when she came clean about her plans.

"I'll keep my hands to myself." He released her and she was suddenly cold and empty without his touch. "For now."

"It's only eight hours." She stifled a smile. "You can last that long without me."

"I went two whole years without you because I was an idiot." His thumb brushed her cheekbone. "I don't want to do that again."

The words sucked the air from her lungs. And judging by his own wide-eyed expression, it wasn't a planned speech.

See, maybe he has *changed. Maybe this is real.*

"I, uh…shower." He shoved his hands into his pockets and turned toward the bathroom.

"That wasn't a real sentence but I'll let you get away with it this time," she teased, trying to play it cool.

But her heart thumped, her blood raced, and the most magical feeling danced along her veins. Gripping the edge of the kitchen counter, she sifted through the facts.

For all the times she'd cursed his name and wiped away tears he'd caused, it hadn't made her want him any less. It hadn't made her want *them* any less. The truth burned bright and furious inside her. She cared about him.

But she wouldn't start a relationship with secrets between them. Tonight, she'd tell him about her plans and hope that he understood why she had to leave Cobalt & Dane. What striking out on her own meant to her.

LOGAN HAD NEEDED a hell of a cold shower to get the thoughts of Addison's naked body out of his mind. That woman had him tangled up worse than a pair of Apple earbuds. Nothing diminished his growing feelings for her—not staying away, not trying to get her out of his system, not confronting his emotions. Nada.

Screw your head back on. The stalker is priority number one. Nothing can happen until you deal with that, because if anything happens to her...

He couldn't even think about what might come next. It was as if his brain simply powered down at the possibility of her being harmed. That meant he needed to regroup and refocus. Everything else could wait.

"Logan?" Emily poked her head into his office. "I've got Rhys and Quinn here to see you."

"Send them in."

His employees entered the room looking like some

funny remake of *The Odd Couple*. Everyone in the office knew they were a tight-knit team but Logan was always struck by how different they were. Rhys was tall, serious and straight as an arrow. He wore a collared shirt and wool suit pants every day. Quinn, on the other hand, was quirky and alternative. Today she had on slashed jeans, a *Legend of Zelda* T-shirt and combat boots. Her highlighter-pink hair hung in a long braid over one shoulder.

"We've got an update on Addison's, uh…" Rhys trailed off.

"Psychotic email acquaintance?" Quinn offered.

"Yes, yes." Logan rolled his hand around. "Go on."

"I'd tasked Quinn with identifying the creator of the Trojan," Rhys said, motioning for Quinn to share what she'd found.

"Right. So, the virus turned out to be a keylogger Trojan. It's a piece of software designed to record keystrokes." Quinn drummed her fingers on her knee as she spoke. "They're mostly used to capture sensitive data like passwords, banking and credit card details, and key identity information such as birth dates, Social Security numbers, et cetera."

Logan frowned. "So he's looking for something specific?"

"I believe so. Using a keylogger means he wants to capture information that's not generally stored in a file or email account. Banking information is definitely the most common target."

"It shouldn't surprise me that this is about money, but why the threatening email?" Logan asked. "If he wanted to access her bank account details why risk the attention? The only reason the email didn't make it to Addison the first time is because of the profanity tripping the filter."

"You're right, if it's about money there's no need for that. Makes me think in this case there's something personal going on," Rhys said. "Quinn was able to trace the name we found in the code to a hacking forum. Turns out DaZetta has been quite busy."

The connection clicked. DaZetta. Michael Zetta. Son of the man Daniel Cobalt had put in jail. The man who'd *died* in jail.

That couldn't be a coincidence.

"I believe he lives in New York." Quinn slid a piece of paper across Logan's desk. "I couldn't confirm his real name, only that the email he used to sign up for his forum account was registered here. I also found an account on Facebook that used the same name and IP address. The address is listed as belonging to a coffee shop in Midtown called Café Mid."

"So we don't have an actual address for him?" Logan asked.

Quinn shook her head. "I'm afraid not. But if he does his business there, then we might be able to hunt him out. There's a chance I could try to get something onto his computer so we can track him, but it's not exactly legal."

"Let's do it the old-fashioned way. Besides, I have an idea how we can figure out his whereabouts."

Logan took a few minutes to fill Rhys and Quinn in on the case he'd come across, which had a link to the name DaZetta. The more he talked it through, the more he was certain Michael Zetta was their guy.

"So what do we do next?" Rhys asked.

"Let's see if we can find a link between DaZetta and Michael Zetta. Anything that ties the two identities together or provides a link to the court case that's going on at the moment." Logan riffled through his files and pulled out the one marked "Vendetti." "The father and son have different surnames, which could possibly mean there is a mother out there who we might be able to press for information, depending on how her relationship with Vendetti ended."

"No mother worth her salt would turn on her son," Quinn said. "Why would this be any different?"

"It's all in how you spin the facts. We might be able to get her to provide information if she feels it will get her son out of hot water," Logan said. "I'll leave it to you two computer whizzes to gather all the technical information, and then if we need to chat with the mother, I'll take care of it. In the meantime, we keep eyes on Addison constantly as well as on the café."

"We should get Addison up to speed." Rhys folded his hands in his lap. "This concerns her directly. She needs to be involved."

Logan nodded. "Agreed. Now that we have more information and an action plan, it's the right time."

Rhys made a face that said he thought the right time had passed. But he didn't comment further.

"Should we call her in?" Quinn asked.

"No." Logan pushed up from his chair. "Leave Addison to me."

ADDISON CRADLED A large coffee cup in her hands while she waited for a reaction from the woman sitting across from her. Penny, her HR manager extraordinaire, sat wide-eyed, processing the information she'd received.

"I never thought you would leave this company," Penny said, sipping her coffee. "Frankly, I'm a bit shocked. I mean, your father was a legend here."

"It's true." Addison nodded, trying to stifle the sharp

pain in her chest that still struck anytime she thought of her dad. "But the one thing I learned from him was that it's possible to build something from scratch. I want that satisfaction, Penny. I want to know what it means to create something yourself and watch it grow. Besides, I'm *positive* this business will be successful. You see how the security guys here couldn't organize paperwork to save themselves."

"It's true." The redhead nodded, a wry smile on her lips. "Owen submitted the files for one of the new hires and forgot to ask the guy to sign his contract. I swear, they have selective attention to detail. If it's for an assignment, they're on point. If it's for HR stuff..." She shook her head.

"I really want you to come with me. I've said from day one you're the best HR person we've ever hired. I need smart, forward-thinking people like you." She sucked in a breath and set her coffee cup down. "I realize this is a bit of a risk for you, but I've planned everything out. This won't be one of those companies that fails because the owner had no idea how to manage the details."

"I don't doubt you at all, Addison. Especially not in that area." Penny paused, her bottom lip drawn between her teeth. There was something more that she wasn't saying.

"Spit it out."

"Have you told Logan? I mean, this company is important to both of you, and I don't want to leave with any bad blood."

Addison raised a brow. "What do you mean?"

"Can I speak frankly?"

"Of course."

"I want to know that you're not trying to poach me to spite him."

Addison blinked. "Excuse me?"

"It's obvious there's something between you two. Everyone can see it, plain as day. Chemistry like that can't be hidden. But I'd hate to think you were only interested in me because it would hurt him." She pressed her lips together. "I just… Please don't take this the wrong way, Addison. I respect you, but I don't want to be caught in the crosshairs."

"It's not like that." She shook her head. "I appreciate your concern, Penn. And Logan doesn't know, but I'm going to tell him soon. I *do* love this company and I want it to succeed with him at the helm. But this whole security business was always Dad and Logan's thing. I never leaned the ropes. And as much as I sometimes hate to admit it, Logan is the better person to run this business because of that. I guess the reason I want to strike out on my own is because I want my skills to be front and center."

"Working in HR, I totally get that. We do always seem to play second fiddle to something more exciting, don't we?"

"Exactly."

Penny tilted her head. "Well, I'd be lying if I said I wasn't tempted. I love working with you."

"The feeling is mutual. But I understand it's a big decision. You don't have to make it now. But I'm meeting with the real estate agent this week about an office space, so things are definitely moving."

"Got it. I won't take too long." Penny stood and picked up her coffee cup. "Thanks for thinking of me."

"You're most welcome."

As Penny exited the coffee shop she walked past Logan. Even from a distance, Addison could see the blush spread across her cheeks. All the girls had a crush on him, even if they were a little scared of his tough managerial persona. But Addison knew the real him; he was a teddy bear underneath it all. A stubborn, pushy one, but a teddy bear nonetheless.

Penny pointed in Addison's direction and when Logan looked over at her it was as if a bolt of lightning shot through her body. What that man could do with a single glance...

"How's my favorite bossy boots?" he said as he sauntered over.

Damn, he looked as tasty as a slice of cherry pie. Fitted dark jeans, black boots and a black-and-white-checked shirt rolled up at the sleeves made him look slick yet relaxed. Addison wondered how hard she'd have to tear at the fabric to make the buttons fly off his shirt.

Get a grip. Fabulous sex will commence in T minus five hours.

"I'm trying to work myself up to tackle the OH&S reports upstairs," she said. "So far, not even coffee is helping."

"Have you got a second to chat?"

"For you," she said, motioning for him to take a seat, "always."

"Maybe we could go for a walk. The coffee might be more effective if you're moving around."

"Unlikely, but it's worth a try." She bundled up her purse and drink and followed him out of the café.

They walked into the sunshine and the hustle and bustle of the Manhattan workday. Addison breathed in the sensory overload—the blare of horns, the scent of pretzels, the warm blast of summer air on her skin. This place was hot and messy. It was noisy and chaotic. But something about that gave her comfort, like the craziness was her blanket. Her shelter. Manhattan was brazen and up-front; what you saw was most certainly what you got.

It reminded her a lot of Logan.

"What did you want to chat about?" she asked, casually linking her arm through his and not caring if anyone from the office might see them. If Penny was right, the cat was not only out of the bag, it had already taken off down the street.

"It's about the guy who's been trying to contact you."

For some reason, the way he said it settled uneasily in her stomach. "Go on."

"We've gained some information on who he might be and I suspect there's a link to one of the cases we looked at on Friday night."

"Oh, well that's good. I guess." She stared ahead as they walked. "Something to go on is a positive thing, right?"

"Yes, it is."

"How did you figure out the connection?"

Logan cleared his throat. "Well, we received another email from him and it contained a virus that we were able to trace. Rhys and Quinn managed to figure out who created the virus and that's when we found the link to one of the old cases."

"I don't remember receiving any more emails. Or did it get caught in the filter again?"

"We'd flagged the email so it wouldn't come to you, just in case it contained any malicious software like this one did." He paused for a moment. "We couldn't risk you accidentally clicking on anything that might put our systems at risk."

With each step she took, Addison's uneasy feeling grew. He was choosing his words carefully, dancing around the truth. He was keeping something from her. "When did the email come in?" She removed her hand from his arm, pausing to look up at him.

"Last week."

She sucked in a breath. "And you thought it would be a good idea *not* to tell me about it until now?"

"I wanted to have a few things in place before I mentioned it."

This was it. The reason she and Logan would never work, because no matter how many times she asked him to view her as an equal, he didn't. Her stomach sank, but she shoved the feeling of sadness to one side. She would not give Logan more opportunities to see her hurting.

"Did it not occur to you that it would be a good idea to inform the person being stalked that her worst nightmare had tried to contact her again? You know, so I could take some precautionary measures?" Sarcasm dripped from her tongue.

"I was with you almost every moment since then."

The words stung as if he'd slapped her across the face. "And here I was thinking you were using the whole 'Mr. Protector' thing to get in my pants."

"Oh, come on."

"Come on what? Is it so fucking hard to understand that I want you to treat me as your partner?" She threw her free hand up into the air, her voice climbing an octave. "Hell, I'd settle for me being treated as well as a client at this point. You keep *them* in the loop, but not your own business partner. Not your own…"

Frustration choked the rest of her words. Were they lovers? Friends with benefits? A future in the making?

Right now it felt like they were strangers.

"Addi, please. Everything I do is in your best interest."

"You do *not* get to decide what is and isn't in my best interest." She jabbed him square in the chest with her pointer finger. "I'm sick of you treating me like some delicate piece of crystal. I won't break at the slightest bump, and the fact that you don't see that is..."

Her chest heaved under her blouse. Everything suddenly felt too tight, her clothes, the air, Logan's presence. She drew in a deep breath, willing her body to calm the hell down. Having a panic attack now would discredit her.

"It's insulting, Logan. I thought you knew me better than that."

"This is exactly *why* I have to look after you. You put your pride before everything else. You're so busy trying to prove your independence that you put yourself at risk."

"Oh, explain to me how I've done that?" People walking past stared at them while they argued, but she didn't give a damn.

"You didn't want us to check your apartment out. I had to argue with you to let us put a simple thing on your computer to make sure he didn't get at you another way. Fuck, Addi. I care about you. Don't you see that?" He raked a hand through his hair. "It's more than that, I—"

"Stop." She held up her hand. "I don't even want to hear what kind of manipulative shit you're going to say next."

His eyes flashed and the muscle worked in his jaw like he was grinding his teeth. "You think I'm manipulative?"

No, she didn't. Not really. But dammit she wanted to

hurt him now; she wanted to make him understand that the way he treated her was wrong. But there wasn't much point. He wouldn't change.

"I'm leaving, Logan." The fight receded within her as quickly as it had bubbled up.

Being angry was an exercise in futility, so she had to pull away. As much as she wanted to be with Logan—and this weekend had certainly planted those seeds of hope—she refused to be treated like a child.

The blood drained from his face, his dark eyes becoming even stormier. "What do you mean you're leaving?"

"I'm leaving Cobalt & Dane to start my own business."

14

ALL POSSIBLE REACTIONS collided within Logan. He wanted to scream, put his fist to a wall. Run. Most of all he wanted to run.

You promised you wouldn't do that again because you're not a goddamn coward anymore.

But the instinct was there, clawing at him. Building up his walls brick by brick. Isolating his heart.

"Don't do this," he said, the weight of his guilt crashing down and suffocating him. He couldn't be the reason she wanted to leave her own company, and if he was…then he'd failed. "Let's take a moment to think about this."

"It's not a rash decision, Logan." Her dark eyes glittered and everything in her demeanor screamed at him to back off, from the crossed arms to the hunched shoulders to the drawn expression. "I've thought it through."

You've done this to her. Again.

"I'm sorry I didn't tell you about the email, but leaving isn't the answer." He tried to reach out to her but she flinched from his hand.

The greatest thing he'd feared was that she would

leave him—like everyone else. Now it was happening before they'd even started, before they'd even had the opportunity to see what they could become. After the incredible weekend they'd spent together, he knew one thing only: that Addison was the most important thing in his life.

Truth was, he'd always known that. Maybe that's was why he was crazy about protecting her, because without Addison he was lost. Incomplete. She was his family, his partner.

His love.

It should have shocked him, but it didn't. The feelings had been there for a decade, whether he'd acknowledged them or not.

"Logan, it's not about the email." She pressed her fingertips to her temple. The sunlight caught the small, clear stone dangling from her ear as she shook her head. "It's been in the works for a while."

For a moment, he thought his chest had been split in two. "How long is *a while*?"

"A few months. More." Her eyes swept over the street, not focusing on anything in particular. Looking anywhere but him. "I don't want to do this anymore. I don't want to be living in your shadow for the rest of my life."

"You don't live in anyone's shadow." His mind spun, desperate for a Band-Aid. Desperate for some way to wind back the past so he could un-fuck this situation. "We can fix—"

"No, we can't. I thought it might work between us, but I was clearly deluding myself." Her eyes glimmered. "I care about you, you know that. But this—" she waved her hand between them "—I'm not doing this anymore.

I'm going out *on my own* and if you have even an ounce of respect for me, you'll let me go."

She'd drawn a line between them and he was screwed either way. If he tried to stop her now, it would prove that he didn't see her as an equal. That he couldn't put her needs before his own. But letting her go would be torture. The company wouldn't be the same without her.

He wouldn't be the same without her.

"I'm walking away now and I don't want you to follow me." She hitched her purse higher up on her shoulder.

"We should still have surveillance on you," he said, swallowing against the lump in his throat. "I'll assign someone else to you."

"I'd appreciate that." She squared her shoulders. It looked as though she might say something else, but instead she turned back toward their office and marched down the street.

Logan shut his eyes for a moment, fighting the urge to race after her. Acting on his emotions had brought him nothing but a world of pain. So, for once, he was going to let his head lead and if that meant he needed to watch her disappear, then so be it.

He pulled his cell from his pocket and dialed Owen's number. "Hey, I need you to take care of something. Find Addi and stick by her all day, okay? I'll fill you in later."

He was going to fix this. No matter what it took, no matter what he had to sacrifice. He would make sure Addison knew what she meant to him.

ADDISON BOUNCED FROM one foot to the other, unsure of what to do. What to say. She'd been home for an hour with Owen. But it wasn't like hanging out with Logan, where she could fully relax. Owen was still her employee.

Sure, he was a friend, but right now she wanted to be alone with her thoughts. Alone to wallow in her misery.

"I can wait outside if you'd prefer," Owen said from where he sat on her couch.

Compared to Logan he was all light—a white shirt, breezy surfer-blond hair and pale denim jeans that matched his eyes. He was funny, slightly irreverent, always at ease. Relaxed and calm.

Here's the problem: you compare everyone *to Logan. And still, even though he screws up at every turn, you think no other man could ever come close to him. Your comparison system is broken.*

"No, it's fine. I don't want you scaring the neighbors."

"*Moi*? Please." He grinned and she could practically see the light reflecting off his perfect teeth. "I'm as harmless as a puppy."

She snorted. "I'm sure you'd like people to believe that."

"It's true. Logan scares everyone enough that I don't need to play the tough guy." He patted the couch beside him. "Why don't we sit and chat? You standing in the kitchen pretending to be busy is kind of weird. I know you're not doing anything."

A laugh bubbled up her throat. "No, I'm not." She opened the fridge and relished the cool blast of air on her skin. "Want a beer?"

"Sorry, doll. I'm on the job. Wouldn't want to disappoint my boss."

Addison grabbed a drink for herself and twisted off the cap. "I'm sure Logan wouldn't mind."

"Firstly, yes he would. He'd kick my ass from here to Canada. Secondly, I was talking about you, Ms. Boss Lady."

She brought the beer bottle up to her lips and tipped her head back. Getting drunk could be the answer—it'd sure helped her last time she'd had issues with Logan. She could drink until she fell down and decided to sleep on the floor.

Yeah, real mature. Dad would be so proud.

"You don't take orders from me," she muttered as she made her way to the couch.

Owen cocked his head. "Sure I do. Nothing better than being bossed around by a gorgeous woman."

"Don't make me spank you."

"Oh, I won't. Not that I wouldn't like to see those little chicken limbs trying to do some damage, mind you." A wicked smile curved on his lips. "But I've known Logan long enough to fear his wrath."

"He doesn't own me." She drew on her beer again, willing the frothy liquid to work its soothing magic.

"No, he doesn't. But cares about you a lot, Addi."

"He's got a funny way of showing it." She plonked her beer bottle down onto the coffee table with an aggressive *clink*. "He keeps secrets, he lies, he pushes me away the second anything starts to feel real." She ticked the items off on her fingers. "And yet he thinks that I should be totally honest with him at all times. It's a two-way street."

Addison clamped her mouth shut when she realized that her voice had shot up to an octave high enough to call the neighborhood dogs to her front door. This wasn't Owen's problem, and she shouldn't be dumping it all on him because he happened to be the unlucky sucker assigned to keep watch over her.

"I'm sorry," she began, but Owen silenced her by holding up his hand.

"It's fine." He squeezed her shoulder. "Logan's a difficult person sometimes. I wouldn't have been able to put up with his control-freak ways over the years if it wasn't for the fact that he's one of the good guys. Everything he does is with the best intentions."

"Intentions don't count for shit if your actions don't stack up," she said with a frown. "If he got out of his own head a little more often, it might be easier to understand him."

"Fair." Owen nodded. "I'm not trying to say he's perfect, because let's be real, he's far from it. But I am saying that you matter to him more than you could possibly understand."

She stared straight ahead, fighting the urge to believe Owen. To let the anger leach out of her body. She couldn't stop being angry, because then she might let herself fall for Logan—harder and faster than ever. Now was not a good time to have her heart broken. Again.

"He'd do anything for you," Owen added.

"Anything except let me live my life."

"Did you know that when your father died, he phoned every florist in the city to find that wreath of yellow roses for the funeral?"

Addison snapped her head toward Owen. "I thought Emily organized that."

"Nope. He remembered that your dad bought you yellow roses every time you argued as a way of saying sorry. And even though there was a rose shortage around the time of the funeral, Logan wouldn't rest until he got that goddamn wreath. He said your dad would have wanted to say sorry for leaving."

Emotion rushed up the back of her throat and she had to choke down a sob. Tears pricked her eyes and she blinked furiously. "No, I didn't know that."

"And when you decided that caffeine was bad for you, Logan made sure we stocked decaf coffee in the kitchen as well as the regular stuff."

"I'd forgotten about that." Against her will, a smile crept across her lips. "I didn't last long on decaf. That stuff is terrible."

"He told me about a year ago that he screwed things up with you after your dad's funeral."

"He told you that?" She reached for her beer and sipped.

"Yeah, he got wasted one night after work. I think the stress of running the company without your dad had finally caught up to him and he went HAM. I got a call from the bartender to come pick him up because he couldn't even stand. Puked his guts up on the side of the street and everything."

"That's unlike him."

"Totally. He was slurring his words something crazy, said he loved you and that he'd ruined everything."

"He said he loved me?" A lump lodged in her throat.

"Sure did, told me a good hundred times before I managed to get him home. I don't think he even remembers me coming to get him that night." Owen chuckled. "But seriously, Addi. I know he isn't always great at expressing himself with words, but he's got the feeling where it counts."

"That's very sage of you, Owen. I had no idea you were such a softy."

"Don't let it get around, okay?" He winked. "I've got a reputation to uphold."

She threw her arm around his shoulder for a brotherly hug. "You sure do."

"So you're going to cut him some slack?"

"I honestly don't know what to do. I feel like every time I get close to him the walls go up and I'm left standing in the cold." Addison rested her head on Owen's shoulder.

Early-evening light filtered into the apartment, catching the sleek glass bowl on her coffee table. Her apartment was like her—carefully presented, stylish. A little impersonal. Guarded.

You think you don't push Logan away, too? You're as scared and self-protecting as he is.

"I want to be in a relationship where I'm equal with my partner—not held up on some untouchable pedestal, but not seen as weak and unable to take care of myself, either." She rubbed her temples with her fingers, trying to ease the tension there. Logan always seemed to get her tied up in knots...even after she'd decided to walk away.

You're hooked on him and walking away won't change that. He makes you feel too good to forget about him.

"And you believe Logan views you as weak?" Owen asked.

"Sometimes. He's confusing as hell. On one hand, I'm this untouchable, perfect thing, and yet on the other he wants to make all my decisions for me." She shook her head. "I've tried talking to him, but he's so stubborn. I can't be someone else's puppet."

"You'll *never* be someone else's puppet, Addi. You're too smart for that."

"I don't think he means to do it, but I went through the same stuff with Dad. Goddamn overprotective men." She huffed. "I want some space from that...just for a while. I need a little room to breathe before I figure out how to tackle Logan."

"Then you won't hear another peep out of me unless

you want to talk about it." Owen made a motion of zipping his mouth closed and throwing away the key.

"You're going to make some girl very happy one day," she said, finishing off her beer. "I'm certain of it."

"Nah." He shook his head, untamed blond hair falling about his eyes. "I don't do relationships. Too messy."

"You're telling me," she muttered, looking out the window as the sun dipped. "I've seen horror movies with less gore."

THE FOLLOWING MORNING, Addison woke with a start. Her sleep had been restless and filled with disturbing dreams. It was as if all the dark thoughts she'd shoved to the corners of her mind had slunk out in the dead of night. Ready to haunt. Ready to terrorize.

She pushed back sweat-dampened hair from her face and let out a long breath. Owen's words were still swirling in her head. Everything he'd said about Logan simmered in her mind, waiting for her to make a decision. The yellow roses had popped up in her dreams, the image of the buttery petals as vivid and real as if she'd been thrown back into the past. Her hand twitched, preparing to reach out and touch the flowers that had comforted her so much on the day she said her final goodbye. Even the memory of how they'd smelled—sweetly reassuring— was in the forefront of her thoughts.

He'd done that. He'd known her well enough to find the one thing that would give her peace on a day where pain was to be irrevocably tattooed onto her heart.

Regret coiled in her stomach like a snake. She'd blown up at him yesterday, perhaps more than was necessary. Sure, he'd done the wrong thing by keeping her out of the loop, but Owen was right. He might not be perfect, but so much of what he did was for her. Maybe they could find a balance between protection and independence.

Addison would always live her own life, be her own person, and if Logan truly did care for her then they would make it work. She could be independent and in love at the same time, without compromising her values.

In love.

The words made butterflies flutter their wings low in her belly. Wasn't love supposed to be sunshine and rainbows rather than passionate arguments? Wasn't love supposed to be easy?

No. Her parents had been very much in love, but they'd argued over much the same things as her and Logan. Safety. Security. Fear. But her parents had loved with a ferocity and wholeheartedness that she'd inherited. That kind of love wasn't easy; it wasn't soft and gentle.

It was rough, jagged. It sat just under the skin.

Was she really in love with Logan? Her fingertips traced the embroidered flowers on her bedspread. Yellow roses.

Yes.

Her body sang with relief at the realization. "I do," she whispered to herself in the quiet of the early morning. "I love him."

But she still had to deal with the issue of her plans. Her business. Love didn't mean giving up on her dreams; she could only hope that Logan would support her to go out on her own, trusting that she would come back to him and be his partner in another way. In a more significant way.

15

"WHERE ARE WE at with Michael Zetta?" Logan leaned back in his desk chair and arranged a mask of calm over his face.

If he'd learned one thing in his life, it was not to let his fear show. But he'd spent the night twisting and turning in his bed, until he'd woken up in a tangle of bedsheets with a pounding in his skull that was loud enough to wake the dead.

He hadn't gone near Addison in two days, not since their fight, and it was killing him.

You would *be near her now if you'd done the right thing and told her what was going on. You've dug this hole; time to bury yourself in it.*

"We weren't able to get eyes on Zetta at the coffee shop," Aiden said, holding his hand up as Logan prepared to bark at him. "But we were able to find out where he worked after tracking him down on LinkedIn. He's employed as an accountant at a small firm in the Financial District."

"Seems odd, then, that he'd be doing his hacking at

a coffee place in Midtown," Rhys commented. "It's not exactly around the corner."

"Could be closer to where he lives?" Aiden shrugged. "Or maybe that's exactly why he chose it, because he wouldn't be recognized there."

"So we've got eyes on him around his work," Logan clarified, eager to keep the conversation on track. "What did we come up with?"

"Not a lot," Aiden admitted, raking a hand through his dark unruly hair. "He seems to lead a pretty normal life. Gets up, goes to work, goes to the gym and comes home. We haven't seen him go into the coffee shop since we started tailing him on Monday."

"It's only been a few days, so we can't count on that to mean anything." Logan drummed his fingers on his knee, his mind trying to fit the pieces of the puzzle together. "Have we got any further information from the tech side?"

"Quinn managed to track down some old posts under the DaZetta username and it turns out he's fairly new to this whole hacking thing," Rhys said. "He had help building the Trojan virus that he sent to Addison. But there's not much else to go on. Her personal computer has come up clean, so we're assuming he doesn't have her other email address."

"I wonder if we could approach him and put the pressure on," Aiden suggested. "He works for an accounting firm. I doubt they'd take too kindly to one of their employees doing some illegal hacking on the side."

"It's worth a try. But it means we'll have to show our hand," Logan said. "Unless you think you can get something more from this virus, Rhys?"

"Unfortunately, no." Rhys shook his head. "I can

only get whatever he gives us at this point, and I'm still confident that he's figured out we're watching since the dummy device won't be sending him any data. Quinn is digging around online to see what else she can find out about him, but it seems he's keeping a fairly low profile. He hasn't posted much on the forum since before the virus came through."

Logan looked over his case notes. "How did things go with the truck that ran Addison off the road?"

"No go," Aiden said. "I checked in with one of my old buddies who's now at the DMV, and we couldn't find any red trucks registered to Michael Zetta. The plate number you gave me is currently unregistered."

"Of course it is." Logan rolled his eyes and pushed up from his chair. "And we didn't get much from the security cameras at the gas station, or from Addison's building security footage. Just a male with dark hair, nothing we didn't already have. Well, if we have someone watching him then let's give it a little longer before we approach Zetta. I want to be sure this is our guy, especially since we haven't got much to tie him to the virus other than a surname, which isn't enough. When we nail him, I want it to stick."

He left his team to keep working and went in search of coffee. Detouring past Addison's office, he noticed she wasn't there and stopped to chat to Renee. Addison's assistant sat behind her desk, which was covered in photos of her adorable twin girls.

"Hi, Logan, what can I do for you?" She smiled brightly as she paused from her lightning-speed typing.

"Where's Addi?" He didn't mean to bark the question out so forcefully, but his nerves were on edge since their fight. Cringing, he tried to smooth his voice out. "I mean, what time do you think she'll be back at her desk?"

"She's sitting in on the finance team meeting at the moment," Renee replied, swiveling toward the second screen on her desk where Addison's calendar sat. "Looks like she'll be in there for at least another half hour. But between you and me, they *always* go over. I think Jeff enjoys hearing the sound of his own voice." She tapped a perfectly manicured finger to her chin. "So I'd give it forty-five to be sure. Would you like me to send her over when she's done?"

"Thanks, Renee, that would be great." He hovered on the spot. "Uh, how is she today?"

Renee raised a brow. "How is she?"

"Yeah, as in..." He cleared his throat. "Mentally."

"Uh, fine, I guess. She looked a little tired this morning but she seemed okay."

"Tired, right." He bobbed his head. Had she been up all night?

An image flitted across his brain—a taunting flash of Addison and Owen together. He gritted his teeth and shoved the thought aside. No, that's not what it would be. She wouldn't jump straight into another man's arms.

Yeah, that's more your move, remember?

"Thanks, Renee."

He headed back to his office and tried to shake the restlessness from his limbs. A feeling of dread plagued him. And that intuition—like an impossible-to-reach itch under the skin—wouldn't let him go.

Something bad is going to happen.

No, it wouldn't. He had to stay on his game, and that meant not letting the dark worries distract him. Addison would be fine. *They* would be fine.

They.

God, how could he have been so stupid? It was a miracle that Addison was still talking to him after everything he'd done. He wouldn't waste that gift. Sure, he couldn't promise that he'd never piss her off in the future by doing what he felt was right, but that wasn't the point, was it? He should have kept her in the loop; he should have talked to her.

Communication. His family had never been good at it.

He hadn't even known his mother was ill until she died. All that time she'd lain there in the hospital, battling complications from her diabetes, he'd been none the wiser. His father had said that he'd wanted to protect Logan from the pain of seeing his mother suffer. But it hadn't done any good. Secrets didn't help anyone.

His mother had been alone—a cheating husband and absent son leaving her to die all by herself, surrounded by beeping machines and strangers in white coats. Pain coursed through him. If only his father had manned up and told him what was going on…

He didn't want to be like his father, which meant he needed to tell Addison how he felt. He needed to promise her that he was ready to be the man she deserved. Honest, open. Trusting.

ADDISON FOUND HERSELF staring off into space while the company's finance director, Jeff, droned on. Normally, she'd be totally engaged in the team meeting. But today her mind was elsewhere.

"Don't you agree, Addison?" Jeff asked from the head of the boardroom table. The rest of the team turned toward her, awaiting her response.

A clock ticked in the silence. The meeting should have ended twenty minutes ago.

"Of course, but, Jeff, I'm afraid I need to run. I've got another meeting that I'm late for." She stood and grabbed her phone, tripping on her chair in her haste to get out of the stuffy room. "Great job, everyone."

Curious eyes stared at her from all around, and she pasted a bright smile on her face before darting out of the room. So what if they all thought she was crazy? No one would say anything to her directly. One of the perks of being the boss, as Logan would say.

Logan. Her tummy flipped as her mind conjured an image of him, but before she could delve too far into the confusing swirl of thoughts in her head, her phone rang.

"Addison Cobalt speaking," she said, pressing the phone to her ear.

"It's Richard James, Comrade Real Estate. I'm calling to confirm our appointment this afternoon." He paused. "I have another buyer who's asking about the property, so I wanted to make sure you're still interested."

"I am," she said resolutely. "I'm leaving the office now."

"Excellent. I'll see you soon."

This was it, the first step in her spreading her wings. If she had the place all lined up before she spoke to Logan, he might take her seriously and not try to convince her to stay at Cobalt & Dane. She could even take him there and explain what it meant to her. She could *show* him how important it was.

Excitement bubbled up in her stomach.

"Addison." Renee waved to catch her attention. "Logan was looking for you earlier. I said I'd ask you to stop by his office when you were done."

"I can't. I've got to run out for an hour or so." Addison sailed past Renee's desk to grab her purse. "Was it urgent?"

"He didn't say." Her assistant cocked her head as she peered at her computer. "Where are you headed?"

Since she'd revealed her secret to the most important person in her life, she wouldn't have to keep her big plans in the shadows for much longer.

Smiling, she straightened her shoulders. "I'm meeting with Richard James from Comrade Real Estate. It's personal…kind of."

"Do you need me to call a car?"

"No, it's okay. I'll grab a cab." She waved over her shoulder as she sailed out of the office, high on the possibilities that lay ahead of her. "I'll be back by three."

By the time Addison made it out of the building and into a cab, her whole body buzzed. It wasn't butterflies in her tummy any longer, but great winged beasts. Dragons, maybe. Something fierce, like her. She stifled a grin, thinking about how proud her father would be. He'd always raised her to be hardworking and creative.

The cab crawled through the city at whatever was slower than a snail's pace. Each block felt like ten, each red light another hurdle to jump. She toyed with her phone, resisting the urge to call Logan. The discussion they needed to have wasn't one that should happen over the phone. They should be face-to-face when she told him that she wanted him. Not for a night or two, but forever.

Hold your horses, Cobalt. Let's tackle one thing at a time—deal with this office space and then think about what to say to Logan.

The cab made it to the bridge and Addison watched

the water rise up to the side. It was a perfect New York summer day—with blistering sunshine and sticky heat. Some people hated it, but she lived for summer. Lived for the freedom that came with tossing all her layers into a cupboard and locking them up for another six months.

She wondered if her new office would have a view, if she'd be able to make it feel cozy and homey.

"We're almost there," the cabbie said as they headed in the direction of Prospect Park.

A guy in a suit stood with a folder on the corner of the street. He waved at the cab as if he recognized her. Funny, since they hadn't met in person. But there were no other cabs around, so she shrugged the thought off.

After paying the fare, she stepped out into the street. "Richard?"

"You must be Addison," he said. She expected him to stick his hand out but he kept a slight distance from her, instead raking his hand through dark hair. "The property is on the other side of the street. We'll need to walk through here."

He gestured to a small lane between two buildings. Unease settled in Addison's stomach, but she looked up at the bright sky and big leafy green trees. It was probably nerves and the weight of her decision settling in.

"Lead the way," she said.

Her heels clicked noisily against the pavement as they walked, echoing down the quiet street. This section of the neighborhood seemed to be peaceful and pretty, exactly what she was searching for. She might even give up her Manhattan apartment for a place closer by—perhaps a cute brownstone. She wondered what Logan would prefer, and then stopped herself.

One step at a time...

The lane became darker as they walked into the shadow of the building next to them. No one appeared to be coming or going.

"Are you sure this is the right way?" Addison asked. She gazed down to a fence at the end of the lane. "It looks like it's closed off."

At that moment Richard turned to her sharply, and she realized he had something in his hand. Fabric. But before she could register what was going on, he had his hand up to her mouth.

Then she faded to nothingness.

16

LOGAN CAME OUT of his office around four to see where Addison had gotten to. It wasn't like her to avoid a meeting, even if she *was* pissed at him. The Addi he knew wouldn't shrink in the face of conflict. He strolled to her office and found Rhys and Quinn chatting with Renee outside.

"She's not back yet," Renee said before he'd even had a chance to open his mouth. Her hair was falling out of its bun and she looked the very definition of frazzled. "I know everyone wants a piece of her time, but I can't magically make her appear."

Logan frowned. "Did she have an appointment somewhere?"

"Yes, but it wasn't in her calendar. Apparently she had a meeting with a real estate company. Comrade Real Estate, I think she said." Renee sighed. "Sorry if I seem snappy, but she promised she'd be back before three, and now I'm trying to rearrange all her afternoon meetings. She won't answer her phone, either."

That didn't sound like Addison at all.

"Can we call Comrade Real Estate?" Quinn suggested. "Maybe her phone died."

Logan nodded. "Yeah, let's do that."

Why would she be meeting with a real estate company? Perhaps after what'd happened she no longer felt safe in her apartment.

"I made a note of the person she was meeting," Renee said. "Richard James. I'll look up the company website and find a phone number."

That prickling unease returned, burrowing under Logan's skin. He tried to dismiss it; Addison was her own person, so she could meet with whomever she wanted about whatever she wanted.

So why did he feel like something was on the verge of going horribly wrong?

"Oh, here we go." Renee picked up her desk phone and dialed the number listed on the Comrade Real Estate website. After a few minutes her eyebrows crinkled. "It's disconnected."

Logan leaned over Renee's shoulder to examine the website. "Is it my imagination or is this the most generic-looking real estate website I've ever seen?"

"You're right." Quinn wrinkled her nose.

After a few clicks around the site they'd learned nothing new about Comrade Real Estate. There were a few headshots of the agents with general bios, but the only number listed was the disconnected one.

"I feel like I've seen this guy before," Quinn said, pointing at Richard James's photo. "He looks so familiar."

Renee dragged the image into a search bar and the man's face popped up several times with different expressions. "It's a stock photo. I recognize him because we used his photo on one of our line management guides."

Rhys shook his head. "Why would they have a stock photo on their website?"

"Check the other images." A sinking feeling settled like a stone in the pit of Logan's stomach.

Sure enough, the other two images also appeared to have been sourced from the same stock image site.

"This doesn't smell good, boss," Quinn said to Rhys with a shake of her head. "Something's not right."

"Okay, let's not panic." Logan held up his hands and drew a long breath so he didn't Hulk-smash a hand through the wall. "Quinn, you check the website out further and see if there's anything else funky about it. Rhys, try tracking Addi's cell phone. And find Aiden and tell him to locate Michael Zetta. Renee, call Addison every few minutes until she picks up."

Everyone went their separate ways. Logan stalked into his office, barely able to suppress the rising fear that churned like foamy black waves in his stomach. As calm as he might appear on the outside, on the inside he was a mess.

Addison was in danger and it was because of him. Because he'd kept her out of the loop. Because he hadn't listened to what she wanted.

He slammed his fist onto his desk and relished the pain as it ricocheted up his arm. "Fucking dammit!"

"Is everything okay?" Emily poked her head into his office, her young face creased with concern. She mustn't have run into Renee yet.

"Addison's missing." He ground the words out, the admission carving pain into his chest. "We're trying to find her."

"Missing?" Emily bit her lip. "How do you know that?"

"She's gone off to meet someone from what appears to be a fake company, and she's not answering her phone." He tried to compose himself, but quieting the noise in his head seemed impossible.

If he lost her now...

"I'm sure she's fine," Emily said. "Maybe she wanted some time to herself. She might have gone shopping."

That showed how little Emily knew about Addison. She put her work before *everything*, which was why he was still reeling from her news that she wanted to strike out on her own.

Before he could respond, his desk phone rang. The screen flashed up "Rhys Glover, IT Dept." "Yes?"

"I've got you on speaker," Rhys said. "Quinn's here. Uh...we have some information."

"Then spit it out," he growled. With his free hand he shooed Emily out of his office, not even caring how much of a prick he must seem.

Nothing mattered more than finding Addison as soon as possible.

"We can't track her phone. It looks like it's been turned off or at the very least disconnected from the internet, so there's no location data being sent," Rhys said.

After a short pause a throat cleared on the other end of the line. "And the IP address for the Comrade Real Estate domain registration matches the one we've been tracking for Michael Zetta," Quinn said.

"Christ!" he roared. "I thought we were supposed to have eyes on that bastard."

It was useless taking the frustration out on his IT team since security detail wasn't their responsibility, but the curse words spewed out of him without restraint. He slammed the phone down and jabbed at the intercom button. "Emily? Tell Aiden and Owen to get their asses in here now."

A moment later, the two men walked into the office. Aiden had a perplexed look on his face. "We've got eyes on Zetta, Logan. I promise, he *doesn't* have Addison with him."

"Then where the fuck is she?" He glared pointedly at Owen. "You were supposed to be watching her."

"Hang on a minute." Owen held his hands up. "She was in the office. Did you expect me to sit on her shoulder like a deranged fucking parrot?"

"If you had, she wouldn't be missing right now." Logan felt the rage boiling away inside him, threatening to burn everything in his wake.

"That's bullshit and you know it." Owen shook his head. "Instead of playing the blame game, we need to figure out what's happened to her. What information do we have?"

Logan filled them in on what Rhys and Quinn had uncovered. "But if Michael Zetta hasn't got her, then who has?"

Two blank faces stared back at him, mirroring the anger and concern that clutched at his own heart. If they didn't think of something soon, he might never get to tell Addison how he felt.

ADDISON TRIED TO suck in a breath, but instead she gagged on something clogging her mouth. Whatever it was, it tasted disgusting—like chemicals and dust and something sweetly metallic that turned her stomach. Her head felt like it weighed a ton and she could barely seem to hold it up.

"Ah, the little princess is *finally* awake." A voice

echoed around the room, the sound bouncing around so much that Addison couldn't tell where it originated. "Did you have a good sleep, my dear?"

Her tongue moved against the material in her mouth and she coughed. If she'd wanted to respond, the sound would have been muffled beyond comprehension anyway. So she stayed quiet.

"It's rude not to answer a question."

Pain blinded Addison as something hard connected with the back of her head and white-hot flashes exploded behind her eyelids. A wet trickle snaked down her skull; she was sure it was blood. She craned her head, trying to see who was behind her.

"You want to look at my face, do you?" The man who'd greeted her with his clipboard came around into her field of vision. "There you are, get your fill."

He didn't look dangerous. His suit was neat, although not flashy, his black hair styled. So ordinary, unassuming. But a gun rested in one of his hands, a telltale smear of blood on the grip.

Danger comes in many forms, her dad had once said to her. She tried to swallow against the rising tide of fear in her throat.

"I should reintroduce myself," he said, his ice-cold eyes piercing in the dull, dusty light.

Addison tried to glance around without letting him out of her peripheral vision. They seemed to be in an abandoned building. Broken windows let in shafts of light; a few pieces of office furniture sat unused and covered in dust.

How far had he taken her?

"You know me as Richard James, but that's only part of the story. I'm Richard James Zetta." Her face must have registered the name, because his lips twisted into a catlike smile. "So you *do* know me. Very clever, Ms. Cobalt. Too bad your security company doesn't seem to be so quick. I believe they've been tailing my brother."

A chill ran through Addison's body. His brother... Michael Zetta. How had they missed that? Logan's team would be following the wrong man, which meant no one would know where she was.

Cold fingers clutched at her heart.

"My stupid, stupid brother. All he cares about is suing the prison." Richard shook his head. "Money doesn't equal justice. It's an eye for an eye! But he's spending everything he has on fancy lawyers and he'll probably lose the lot. But you—" he pointed at her with the gun "—you can help me get justice for my father."

She tried to speak, but the words were lost in her gag. Her voice sounded muffled and her throat burned.

"Shh." He held up a finger. "It's not your turn, Addison. I'm sure you're not used to having someone tell you what to do, but you're smart enough to understand how this works. You do what I say and I don't shoot you. Got it?"

She nodded, shivering at the cold grip of fear's bony fingers wrapping around her spine.

"Now, we're going to have a little game of show-and-tell. I show you your bank's website and you tell me how to access your accounts." He cackled at her confused look. "Money doesn't equal justice for me, but I don't want my brother going broke trying to pay legal fees. I figure you can help us both get what we want."

The money didn't matter to her, but it was clear that nothing she handed over would save her. She struggled against the restraints, trying to get a better view of the room. Trying to see if there was some way she could escape.

"And before you start thinking that your employees might turn up looking for you, don't bother." Richard held up a broken device that appeared to be her smartphone. "I made sure no one would be able to track you."

~~Her stomach sank.~~ How the hell was she going to get out of this?

"WE'VE MISSED SOMETHING," Logan said as he faced the best and brightest of his team. Rhys, Quinn, Aiden and Owen all looked among one another, but no one seemed to have any ideas. "What is Zetta's current position?"

"He's at work," Aiden replied, tapping away at the laptop in front of him. They all sat around the boardroom table with their computers, desperately clutching at anything that might help them find Addison. "I've checked in with our eyes on the ground and he hasn't left the building so far today."

"He must be working with someone else," Owen said. "What about a relative of his father? Have we seen any other names come up in the court case against the prison?"

"Not that I could find," Quinn replied, blowing a stray strand of hot-pink hair out of her eyes. "We looked into the mother, but I found an obituary for her. Maria Zetta died last year. I also went through a bunch of articles about the case and the only person listed was Michael Zetta."

"And there were no other relatives listed in the obituary?" Logan asked.

"Let me bring it up. I don't remember seeing anything else." Quinn cocked her head. "All it says is that it was written by the 'Zetta family.'"

"Maybe there's another obituary?" Rhys said, leaning over to read Quinn's screen.

Soft clicking filled the room as they searched, the minutes ticking away faster than Logan could stand. "Here we go," Quinn said. "There was another obituary posted a few days later. It says, 'Maria is survived by her two sons.' So Michael must have a brother."

"Find him," Logan growled. "Aiden, get in touch with your man on the ground and tell him that we may need to approach."

Aiden nodded and left the room, tapping at his phone as he walked.

"Look for school records," Rhys said to Quinn. "We might be able to find the brother's name through school sporting teams or academic achievements."

The room was suddenly a flurry of activity, everyone suggesting ways to find the other Zetta brother. A few seconds later Quinn gasped. "I found something. Michael Zetta played tennis for his high school all the way until his senior year."

"And his brother played, too?" Logan asked.

"No." She glanced up, her hazel eyes wide. "But someone from Cobalt & Dane did."

She turned her laptop around to show an old photo of a boy and girl in tennis whites. They had matching jet-black hair and confident smiles. The names printed under the photo were Michael Zetta and Emily Facinelli.

Logan's heart twisted in his chest as he stared at the photo. She looked much younger in the photo, but he would recognize his assistant anywhere.

"Everybody clear out," he said, trying to keep his voice from shaking. "Emily and I need to have a chat."

17

"WHERE IS SHE?" He braced both hands on the surface of the table, more to stop himself from trembling with rage than to intimidate his pint-sized assistant, Emily.

Right now, controlling himself was taking up all his mental energy, which left little for dealing with this situation calmly.

"I don't know what you're talking about." She stared up at him with large eyes. Her lips were pulled taut and her hands were folded in her lap.

"You're telling me you have no idea where Addison is currently?"

"Why would I know where she is? I don't take care of her schedule." She picked at the hem of her black pencil skirt, her brow crinkled. "Ask Renee."

"Okay, fine. Let's try this." He showed her the copy of the photo from earlier. "Who are the people in this photo?"

"That's me," she said, her voice suddenly wavering. "And that's my best friend, Michael. We play mixed doubles together." She paused. "Why do you have an old photo of me?"

"Does Michael have a brother?" The pieces were starting to fall into place, his body buzzing with the possibility that he could make it all right again. That he could save Addison.

Emily nodded. "Yes, he has a brother named Richard."

"And where does Richard work? It's important that you tell me, Emily."

"Umm." She bit down on her lip. "He was doing some cleaning work for a real estate company. Something to do with building maintenance... I'm not quite sure."

"Was the company called Comrade Real Estate?"

"I don't think so." She shook her head. "But I can't remember the name. It was one of the big companies, I think. He was excited when he got the job because he'd been looking for work on and off for over a year without much luck."

"It's very important I find out where he works, Emily. Could you call Michael and find out?"

"Why? What's going on?" She shook her head. "I don't see what it has to do with Addison."

"We think he's kidnapped her and may intend to harm her." Saying the words caused his throat to tighten, a lump lodging in his windpipe and blocking anything further from coming out.

"Oh God." She pressed her hand to her cheek.

Logan nodded and swallowed slowly, taking back control of his body. Now was not the time to let emotion take over; he had to treat this like any other assignment. Stay calm, stay focused. Get the client out alive.

But this wasn't any other client. This was the woman he loved. And he would get her out alive.

"Okay, of course I'll call Michael." Emily jumped up from her chair. "I'll do it right now."

REGRETS RIOTED IN Addison's mind. She should have taken that first email more seriously; she should have listened to Rhys and Logan. She should have at least told someone where she would be. But the chances of anyone finding her now...well, they were wafer-thin.

"I have to confess, this is so much more satisfying than I thought it would be." Richard Zetta looked her over, his eyes gleaming in a way that made her skin crawl. He had a laptop resting on an old desk and he typed with one hand since his other hand was occupied by the gun. "I can only hope there is an afterlife so your father can see what he's done to you."

Her eyes watered as she tried to scream through the cotton gag. It was useless, of course, since they were alone in a big, empty building. But she couldn't go down silently. She *wouldn't*.

"Do you think I wanted to do this?" Richard asked, his eyes wide and bulging. "No, I wanted my father home. He would never have hurt anyone. He was taking from rich people who had more money than sense so he could pay for my brother and me to go to college."

Addison squeezed her eyes shut, willing the plastic ties binding her to fall away. But as she wriggled, they burned into her skin. The harsh edges cut her, leaving her skin raw and probably bleeding.

"Don't shut your eyes!" He hit her again, this time across the cheek, and her head whipped back as the chair rocked.

It teetered and then fell. But there was nothing she could do to brace her fall and she landed hard against the concrete. The pain stole her breath as it shot up her arm like fireworks. Her whole body was ablaze.

"You're not allowed to ignore me." He kicked her in the rib cage, piling on more hurt. More pain. "No one is allowed to ignore me anymore because *I* am the one avenging my father."

Her throat prickled, warm tears seeping out the edges of her eyes as she lay there bound and immobile. If this was going to be the end, she hoped it would come swiftly. And she hoped, more than anything else, that Logan would somehow know how she felt about him. That she loved him and had done so ever since she was a besotted teenager.

Richard continued to rage at her, but Addison blocked out the sound. She may not know the right way to get out of zip ties, but her mind was her best feature. In that aspect, she was stronger than most. She wouldn't crumble. She had to *think*.

Her tongue worked at the gag, trying to push it out of her mouth. Or at the very least, slip it over her lip so that she could get some words out. Without the ability to speak she was at a disadvantage. Rubbing her face against the ground, the fabric rolled out of her mouth.

"Richard, please." She managed to say the words but her voice was weak and croaky. How long had she been out? "This isn't going to bring your father back."

"It's not about bringing him back," he snapped. "It's about doing what's right."

He seemed to calm down and refocus. From her angle on the ground she could see him move back toward the desk, and a moment later the clicking of keys resumed.

"And you think hurting me is going to make you feel better? News flash, it won't." She glared up at him from her curled position on the floor.

"Oh it will." He looked down to her. "Okay, we're going to start with your customer identification number."

A sharp, stabbing pain started radiating outward from her arm and midsection. Something wasn't right, a broken bone, maybe. Bruising, possibly internal bleeding. She forced down the swell of nausea in her stomach.

The second she gave him her banking account details she was as good as dead.

"Nothing will ever make those feelings go away," she said, stalling. "Do what you will, but I promise you that even if you kill me it won't make the pain and guilt and grief any better. And I'm guessing you know that already."

He crouched down, resting the gun inches from her head. She could see straight down the black barrel, like it was some rabbit hole into another life. As she waited for the beginning of the end, Addison's heart pounded hard in her chest. Fighting to stay alive, fighting to fuel her with energy that she had no way of expending.

"Richard Zetta!" His name echoed through the empty room, like a gunshot bouncing off the walls. "Step back and keep the gun where I can see it."

For a moment Addison wondered if her imagination had taken over and dreamed Logan into existence. Her white knight, as much as she'd always resented him for trying to play that role, was here for her. His footsteps sounded slow and steady as he approached. She even recognized that about him, the careful way he walked. With purpose, with intent.

Richard gripped the gun tighter, his knuckles white. "Well, well, if it isn't Logan Dane."

"I don't have any beef with you," Logan said in calm, soothing tones. "But I can't let you hurt her."

She still couldn't see him, but his presence filled the air. It breathed hope into her lungs.

"I'll shoot her if you come any closer." Richard waved the gun around but it was clear he'd been spooked. Obviously he had no contingency plan for being discovered. He was alone, whereas Logan would definitely have backup.

"Do I need to call my team in here or will you let her go?" Logan's voice was honey smooth, as calm as if he were ordering a drink at a bar. No aggression, no fear. He'd done this before and he knew that unnecessary emotion wouldn't help. He'd told her that once.

"This is not your place," Richard spat, and he moved to point the gun at Addison.

There was a *click*, footsteps. More people had entered the room. "We'll take you down before you even get a shot off, Richard. Lower the gun and we can all walk away." Logan stepped closer, his boots coming into Addison's line of sight.

She tried to move but pain engulfed her and she muffled a cry.

"Are you okay, Addi?" he asked as he stepped forward. His boots were covered in the dust that coated the floor, which now lined her throat and lungs.

She coughed. "Yeah, mostly."

"Fuck both of you," Richard screamed. "I know who you are, and you're as bad as she is."

"We're just doing our jobs," Logan said calmly. "Put the gun down."

In the distance Addison could see another set of feet moving quickly, quietly. Like a ninja. *Owen.* Richard hadn't noticed anyone coming up behind him because

Logan had his full attention. They must be hoping not to shoot him by catching him unawares.

"You think I won't pull the trigger?" Richard aimed the gun back down at Addison and she instinctively cringed, clamping her eyes shut. "You think I won't kill her?"

"If you'd wanted to kill her you would have done it already." Logan took another step and then another. "I know you're angry and grieving. But this isn't the way to fix that."

Before Richard had the chance to respond, Owen sneaked up behind him and got one bulky arm around his throat. With his other hand he directed Richard's hand away from her. A shot went off, shattering a window. Glass flashed as it fell to the ground in twinkling shards, the sound echoing around the room.

Aiden rushed Richard and retrieved the gun from him, disarming him and immediately dumping the cartridge out onto the floor with a loud *clang*.

"Are you hurt?" Logan dropped to the floor in front of her, his hands smoothing over her face.

"My arm." She cringed as the pain intensified. "And my head."

Now that Richard was no longer a threat, all the pain came back in full, vibrant feeling. Her head pounded like someone was taking a sledgehammer to the inside of her skull. Each breath was like jabbing a thousand needles into her lungs.

Logan gingerly slipped his hands under her arms and helped to lift her off the ground, setting the chair down first. He dug a Swiss army knife out of his pocket and cut the ties from her wrists, then her ankles. While he worked, she saw a billowing anger in his eyes. The

dark brown depths—usually so warm and sensual—
were wild.

"The police are on their way," Aiden announced.
"We'll hold Richard here until they're ready. Paramed-
ics should be here shortly."

Addison twisted her good wrist, not daring to even try
to move her other arm. "How did you find me, Logan?"

"*We* found you. It was a team effort." He grabbed her
hand and wrapped it over his arm, bracing her as she
stood slowly. "But I can tell you right now, I would have
ripped through every building in this city to find you."

He filled her in on the connection between the Zettas
and Emily as they walked slowly out of the building.
Apparently Michael had given her the name of the
company Richard was working for, as well as the fact
that his brother been assigned to clean an abandoned
building—it had sounded like the perfect spot to commit
a crime. Addison didn't even want to think about what
might have happened if they'd gone to the wrong place.

For now, she needed to focus on something other than
her pain and fear lest she collapse in an emotional heap.
It wouldn't do to let the team see her as some damsel in
distress, even though that's exactly how she felt.

"We're a good team, you and I," he said as they
stepped out of the gloomy building and into the fading sunlight.

"Why, because I always need saving and you have a
hero complex?" she quipped. Jokes were easier than the
truth right now, although what she'd said was certainly
colored with experience.

"It was a general observation." He brushed the hair
back from her face and she felt the grit of dirt and dust
slide along her scratched-up skin. "We've built a good

company together. We've taken what your father started and made it stronger. Better."

The last thing she needed right now was a guilt trip about her decision to leave. This event hadn't changed her mind. If anything, it only made her more determined to strike out on her own. Life was short and psychos were aplenty.

She had to live her life to the fullest, corny as it sounded. She could see that now. There was no point holding back, no point being fearful. Because even the most cautious people could get caught up in danger.

"I was wrong not to listen to you," she said as they sat on a stone wall outside the building, waiting for the ambulance to arrive. Her arm throbbed and she cradled it against her chest. "This could have been avoided if I'd taken your advice."

"And I could have been less of an asshole about it." He leaned his head against her, the familiar scent of his soap cutting through the grime clogging her throat and nostrils. Even with all that filth, she could still feel him. Sense him.

No matter how at odds they were, his presence was a comfort.

"This could have ended very differently," she whispered, realization creeping into her mind. "You could have found me with a bullet between the eyes."

"I know." His hand found her good one, his fingers interlocking with hers.

"I don't want to play games anymore, Logan." She blinked as a wave of emotion crashed over her, threatening to pull her under its dark, endless depths. "I want us to be real with each other. No more power struggles, no more cat and mouse."

"I kind of like the cat and mouse." A smile tugged on his lips.

"I'm still leaving Cobalt & Dane."

The wail of sirens filled the air, growing louder with each passing second. Soon she would be patched up, shiny as new. But she wouldn't forget today—what she might have lost. What she might have thrown away because of her own stubbornness.

"I understand," he said, his head bobbing. "And I support you no matter what."

18

WHEN ADDISON WOKE, her eyes felt like they were filled with grit. She lifted a hand to rub them, but her arm refused to move and pain shot straight up to her shoulder. That's when she noticed the plaster and sling.

Oh right, the doctor had said she had a broken arm. Bruised ribs. Stitches. Possible concussion.

The last one must have been okay since she'd woken up from her sleep. She blinked, trying to bring the room into focus. White on white on white. Her stomach roiled.

"Goddamn hospitals," she muttered, though her voice was merely a croak.

She hadn't set foot in one since her father had passed away. Something about the smell seemed to bring the memories rushing back, and with it feelings of hopelessness and despair. She'd never felt more useless in all her life than she had when she'd sat at her father's side and watched him slowly die.

Tears pricked at her eyes but she didn't even have the energy to cry. Her head sank back into the pillow. The room was silent. Everyone from Cobalt & Dane must have gone home, but she'd been hoping that Logan might still be here.

That he might care enough to be by her side when she woke, even though she'd told him she still planned to leave.

A hot, wet droplet fell onto her cheek and rolled toward her jaw. Her throat tightened as she tried—and failed—to stem her emotions. As she shut her eyes, a scent caught her attention. Something sweet...familiar.

Reaching with her good hand, she found the remote for the bed and pushed the button that would help her sit up. That's when she caught sight of them.

Yellow roses. Everywhere.

Not just one pretty bunch in a vase, but multiple bunches. The room was a florist's dream. There were bright blooms the color of lemon rind, rich bold bursts of gold, and pale muted petals in tones of butter and early-morning sunshine. Some sat in boxes, ringed with delicate white baby's breath, and others were left alone, allowed to shine all by themselves.

A sob caught in her throat. Logan.

He was carrying on a tradition, letting his actions speak louder than his words. A smile tugged at her lips and, as if on cue, he walked into the room. Another box of flowers bundled up in his arms.

"What on earth are you doing?" She brushed the fallen tears away with her good hand.

"I had to pick these up," he grumbled, setting them down on one of the few free spots remaining. "They called me last minute to tell me the delivery guy was sick."

"Did you buy all of them?" she asked, although she

already knew the answer. When he nodded she laughed. "Why?"

"I have a lot of things to apologize for." The statement was matter-of-fact, spare. Logan was a man who owned his mistakes and she respected him for that. "I got one lot of flowers for every apology, since I figured I'd already fallen behind by not saying anything for the past few years."

"Let's hear it then." She patted the bed. "I won't say no to an apology."

"You're one of a kind, you know that, right?" His dark eyes gleamed. The bed creaked under his weight as he sat, his large frame encased in an inky black T-shirt that looked harsh against the clinical white furnishings. "Addi, I'm sorry for being such a jerk."

He reached for her hand and ran his thumb over her knuckles. The gentle touch sent a shiver rocketing through her, blanking out everything else—the pain, uncertainty. Grief.

"I respect that you want to be independent and that you want your space." His eyes seemed to look past her. "I've had too much of a hand in your life where you didn't want me."

"I do want you in my life," she said, squeezing his hand. "But I want to be my own person at the same time."

"I get it." He nodded. "It's just that the thought of anything happening to you…it fucking terrifies me. The world is so much better with you around. *I'm* so much better with you around."

"What are you trying to say?"

When he glanced up, every bone in her body melted under the intensity of his gaze. There was a raw openness in his expression that she'd never seen before.

"I want us to be Cobalt & Dane again."

Disappointment clutched at her heart like a tight fist. "What happened doesn't change my plans, Logan. I want to go out on my own and try to make it. I want to build something and see if it survives. I want—"

"Stop." He shook his head. "What I meant is that I want us to be together again. Not as a company but as a…" He swallowed. "I don't know, just…us."

"You mean, like in a relationship?" A smile melted across her lips. "An exclusive relationship?"

"I mean forever." He reached out and brushed a thumb over her cheek, touching one of the cuts there. The gesture was so soft, so tender. "With a ring and everything. I don't want to keep pretending that you're not the best thing in my life because I'm scared to lose you."

They were the words she'd longed to hear from him, words that he whispered to her in the quiet corners of her dreams. But this wasn't a dream.

Her hands found his face; they traced the rough angle of his jaw—now coated in stubble—and the high planes of his cheekbones. She wanted to memorize him with her hands, capture this moment in her mind so that she could replay it over and over and over.

"I'm not going anywhere. Scout's honor." She saluted him and he chuckled.

The room hummed around them. Machines beeped, footsteps rushed past, and the hustle and bustle of the hospital crackled in her ears like white noise. None of it mattered—not her broken bones or her scarred heart. Not all their collective fears and mistakes.

They were together now and they were laying themselves bare.

"I get that you might leave me." He nodded, his eyes

down as if he were sorting something out in his head. She brushed her fingers through his hair. "You might get sick or I might get sick. It might happen unexpectedly but…that's not a reason to keep us apart."

"Or we might grow old and gray and wrinkly together. That's an option, too."

"I'd like that." His eyes shone as he lifted them to hers. "But only if you promise you won't stop wearing all that sexy underwear, even if we do get old."

She grinned. "You have my word."

He leaned forward to kiss her, being careful not to put pressure on her injured arm. But right now, Addison couldn't care less about her scars. About her pain. She had Logan, and that was all that mattered.

As his lips brushed hers the world melted away. Her body sang at his touch. His kiss was better than any medicine, any drug. He was hers, and now she was whole.

"I love you," she said as they pulled apart, his taste still lingering on her lips. "And I have for a very long time."

"Couldn't resist my brooding charms, eh?" He flashed her that roguish smirk that she loved so very much.

"Not even a little bit." She touched his kiss-bruised mouth. "No matter how frustrated I got with you poking around in my life, I could never stay away from you. You've got a good heart, Logan. You're a good man. *My* man."

"I love you, too." He cupped her face. "You're my family, Addi. You're my best friend, my voice of reason."

"Your future wife," she whispered.

"My future everything."

Epilogue

Three months later

LOGAN STOOD TO the side of the room, trying to figure out how to get the beer up to his mouth without splitting the too-tight fabric of his costume around his biceps. Addison had insisted that the Batman costume should fit like a second skin, otherwise the fantasy would be ruined, apparently. And since she was pouring herself into a latex Catwoman costume, it was only fair that he come to the party—both literally *and* figuratively.

"You been working out, Logan? Looks like you're about to Hulk out of that costume." Owen said as he sauntered over with Aiden, looking free and breezy in what appeared to be a white bedsheet. Gold leaves glinted against his blond hair, and a thin rope cinched in his waist. "Do I need to be on wardrobe malfunction watch?"

"Very funny," he grumbled. "At least I'm wearing a costume."

"What's that supposed to mean?" Owen looked down at himself. "This is a genuine Roman-era bedsheet."

"Genuine, huh?" Aiden tugged at the care label sewn into the fabric knotted at his friend's waist.

"Totally." Owen grinned. "Besides, this is the perfect costume for me."

"Because you like easy access?" Aiden tossed his head back and laughed.

"Because I like history. What does your costume say about you?" He gestured to Aiden's bright blue overalls and comically fake mustache.

"It's an inside joke." Aiden adjusted the red cap on his head, which had the letter *M* emblazoned on it. "She was supposed to dress up as Princess Peach, but we agreed that Lara Croft suits her better."

They looked over to where Quinn stood in the iconic costume, her pink hair hanging in a long braid down her back. She was laughing at something Rhys had said. He and his girlfriend, Wren, were dressed as *Big Bang Theory* characters.

"This whole thing is so Quinn, isn't it?" Owen commented. "Of course she would have an engagement party that resembles a nerd convention. But I still can't believe she said yes to you."

"Why wouldn't she?" Aiden puffed out his chest, which only served to make him look even more ridiculous in his Super Mario outfit. "We're perfect together."

"Someone pass me a bucket," Owen joked, slapping Aiden on his back. "You make me sick."

Logan shook his head and forced the beer up to his lips, cringing when the seams of the Batsuit protested. In front of him, the room was filled with people in colorful costumes. It was hard to recognize most of the people, although his eyes were inexorably drawn to Addison's slim body encased in a reflective black catsuit. A headband with black cat ears perched on top of her blond hair. She toyed with a whip as she talked to a woman in a Princess Leia costume who cradled a noticeable baby bump. Beside them, Max Ridgeway—his former staff member—talked animatedly, his broad Australian accent carrying easily across the room.

"Looks like it'll be your turn next." Owen dug his elbow into Logan's ribs. "Max and Rose will be having their baby in a few months, and Rhys and Wren are already planning their wedding. Now these two knuckleheads are getting hitched as well."

A few months ago, Owen's comment would have had him running for the hills. Back then, marriage and relationships had been synonymous with loss. Disappointment. Devastation. But Addison had helped him change those views.

Across the room, her eyes found his and a saucy smile crept over her lips. One too many looks like that and he'd be hauling that latex-covered ass out of the party and back to their apartment.

Their apartment.

The thought of their new, shared home made him want to grin like a fool. The little brownstone in Brooklyn was so different from what either of them had lived in before. It was a blend of both their personalities—from the girlie perfumes on her nightstand to the vintage fishing rod that hung in the living room. It'd belonged to her father, and she'd cleaned it up as a housewarming present for him.

There was a vase on the coffee table that he always stocked with fresh yellow roses. Because mistakes were aplenty, and he never again wanted to fall behind in apologizing.

Marriage might be in the cards at some point in the future, if they both wanted it. But for now he was content to make up for lost time with Addison. They had years of pent-up attraction to feast on, and he wasn't going to waste a single moment with her. Especially since he didn't get to see her around the office anymore now that she'd officially launched her business.

"What about you?" Logan turned the question around. "You're next in line."

"I'm immune to whatever virus you guys all seem to have caught," Owen said with a cavalier shrug. "It's probably for the best. I've got plans to get Marilyn Monroe's number before the night is out." He winked at the woman in the blond wig and white dress standing a few feet away, and she blushed.

"You'll change your mind when the right woman comes along," Logan said, his eyes locked onto Addison as she broke away from her conversation and made her way over to him.

"What if she's already been and gone?" Owen said darkly. The words were so soft, Logan wondered if they were a figment of his imagination.

But before he could question Owen further, Addison sidled up next to him and wrapped a black gloved hand around his waist. Her blond hair was a stark contrast to the all-black outfit and dark, smudgy makeup.

"Meow," she said with a grin. "Having fun?"

"I'd be having more fun if we were at home." He leaned down to capture her mouth in a deep kiss. No matter how many times he kissed her, desperation always stirred deep in his chest. How had he even been able to stay away from her for so long? "I'm going to tear that costume off with my teeth."

"I can't wait. It's hot as hell in here."

"I was asking Logan when you two were going to get hitched," Owen interjected with an evil grin. "Seems to be the thing to do around here."

"There's no rush." Addison's eyes gleamed as she looked at up Logan. "I've got everything I could possibly want in my life right now. I'm one happy cat."

Logan brushed his lips over Addison's forehead. "Now we have to make sure I don't screw anything up."

"Little mistakes are okay, especially if we get to have makeup sex." She reached behind him and squeezed his butt. "I can be very forgiving like that."

"I can't. I don't ever want to screw up again." He leaned his forehead against hers and the rest of the party faded away—all the people, the sounds, the colors. Gone. "I don't ever want to hurt you again."

"You won't, Logan. We've got our agreement, remember? We don't sweep things under the rug, we don't keep secrets, and we don't sleep on an argument." Her palms cupped his face. "We don't run."

"We don't run," he repeated. Then a naughty thought crept into his head. "Well, we *could* run just this once. I'm betting a couple of ice cubes would feel pretty damn good after being cooped up in that suit."

"I bet we don't make it home before you start tearing my clothes off." Her eyes glinted. "And this suit is one piece, Logan. You're going down this time."

He slipped his hand into hers and tugged her toward the door. "You're on."

* * * * *

COMING NEXT MONTH FROM

HARLEQUIN *Blaze*

Available February 21, 2017

#931 SIZZLING SUMMER NIGHTS
Made in Montana • by Debbi Rawlins
Rancher Seth Landers is striving to rebuild his family's trust and his place in the community. Beautiful visitor Hannah Hastings has her own agenda. Will she be his greatest reward...or his biggest downfall?

#932 TEMPTED
by Kimberly Van Meter
Former air force pilot Teagan Carmichael is maneuvered into going on a singles cruise, where he meets Harper Riley, the sexiest woman he's ever seen. There's only one problem—she's a con artist.

#933 HER HOLIDAY FLING
Wild Wedding Nights • by Jennifer Snow
Hayley Hanna needs a fake fiancé for her corporate retreat, and Chase Hartley is perfect—he's sexy, funny and kind—but it's just a business deal. That means no kissing, no sex and *no* falling in love!

#934 A COWBOY IN PARADISE
by Shana Gray
In her designer dress and high-heeled shoes, Jimi clearly didn't belong on a dusty Hawaiian ranch. Or with rugged cowboy Dallas Wilde. Dallas may be a delicious temptation, but could a city girl ever trade Louboutins for lassoes?

HBCNM0217

*Hannah Hastings is just looking for a hot vacation fling.
Can fun-loving and downright gorgeous rancher
Seth Landers tempt her to stay forever?*

*Read on for a sneak preview of
SIZZLING SUMMER NIGHTS,
the latest book in Debbi Rawlins's much loved
MADE IN MONTANA miniseries.*

"I think the best we can hope for is no rocks." Seth nodded to an area where the grass had been flattened.

"This is fine with me," she said, and helped him spread the blanket. "What? No pillows?"

Seth chuckled. "You've lived in Dallas too long."

Crouching, he flattened more of the grass before smoothing the blanket over it. "Here's your pillow, princess."

Hannah laughed. "I was joking," she said, then pinned him with a mock glare. "Princess? Ha. Far from it."

"Come here."

"Don't you mean, come here, please?" She watched a shadow cross his face and realized a cloud had passed over the moon. It made him look a little dangerous, certainly mysterious and too damn sexy. He could've just snapped his fingers and she would've scurried over.

"Please," he said.

She gave a final tug on the blanket, buying herself a few seconds to calm down. "Where do you want me?"

"Right here." He caught her arm and gently pulled her closer, then turned her around and put a hand on her shoulder. "Now, look up. How's this view?"

Hannah felt his heat against her back, the steady presence of his palm cupping her shoulder. "Perfect," she whispered.

His warm breath tickled the side of her neck. He pressed his lips against her skin. "You smell good," he murmured, running his hand down her arm. With his other hand he swept the hair away from her neck. His breath stirred the loose strands at the side of her face.

Hannah was too dizzy to think of one damn thing to say. She saw a pair of eerie, yellowish eyes in the trees, low to the ground. Then a howl split the night. She stifled a shriek, whirled and threw her arms around Seth's neck.

He enfolded her in his strong, muscled arms and held her close. "It's nowhere near us."

"I don't know why it made me jumpy," she said, embarrassed but loving the feel of his hard body flush with hers. "I'm used to coyotes."

"That was a wolf."

Wolf? Did they run from humans or put them on the menu? She leaned back and looked up at him. Before she could question whether or not this was a good idea, Seth lowered his head.

Their lips touched and she was lost in the fog.

Don't miss
SIZZLING SUMMER NIGHTS
by Debbi Rawlins, available March 2017 wherever
Harlequin® Blaze® books and ebooks are sold.

www.Harlequin.com

SPECIAL EXCERPT FROM

HQN™

Single mom Harper Maclean has two priorities—raising her son and starting over. Her mysterious new neighbor is charming and sexy, but Diego Torres asks far too many questions…

Enjoy a sneak peek of CALL TO HONOR, the first book in the new SEAL BROTHERHOOD series by Tawny Weber.

Harper stepped outside and froze.

Diego was in his backyard. Barefoot and shirtless, he wore what looked like black pajama bottoms. Kicks, turns, chops and punches flowed in a seamlessly elegant dance.

Shirtless.

She couldn't quite get past that one particular point. But instead of licking her lips, Harper clenched her fists.

She watched him do some sort of flip, feet in the air and his body resting on one hand. Muscles rippled, but he wasn't even breathing hard as he executed an elegant somersault to land feet first on the grass.

Wow.

He had tattoos.

Again, wow.

He had a cross riding low on his hip and something tribal circling his biceps.

Who knew tattoos were so sexy?

Harper's mouth went dry. Her libido, eight years in deep freeze, exploded into lusty flames.

The man was incredible.

Short black hair spiked here and there over a face made for appreciative sighs. Thick brows arched over deep-set eyes, and he had a scar on his chin that glowed in the moonlight.

Harper decided that she'd better get the hell out of there.

But just as she turned to go, she spotted Nathan's baseball.

"You looking for the ball?" His words came low and easy like his smile.

"Yes, my son lost it." She eyed the distance between her and the ball. It wasn't far, but she'd have to skirt awfully close to the man.

"Good yard for working out," he said with a nod of approval. He grabbed the ball, then stopped a couple of feet from her.

"I should get that to Nathan." She cleared her throat, tried a smile. "He's very attached to it."

"The kid's a pistol." His eyes were much too intense as he watched her face.

That's when she realized what she must look like. She'd tossed an oversize T-shirt atop her green yoga bra and leggings. Her hair was pulled into a sloppy ponytail, and she wore no makeup.

"Thanks for finding it."

His eyes not leaving hers, he moved closer.

Close enough that his scent—fresh male with a hint of earthy sweat and clean soap—wrapped around her.

Finally, he placed the ball in her outstretched hand. "Everything okay?"

No. Unable to resist, she said, "Why do you ask?"

"I don't like seeing a beautiful woman in a hurry to get away from me." The shadows did nothing to hide the wicked charm of his smile or the hint of sexual heat in his gaze.

It was the same heat Harper felt sizzling deep in her belly.

Thankfully, the tiny voice in her mind still had enough control to scream, "Danger."

"I'm hurrying because I don't like to leave my son inside alone," she managed to say. "Again, thanks for your help."

And with that, she slipped through the hedge before he could say another word. It wasn't until she was inside the house that she realized she was holding her breath.

What's next in store for Harper, Diego and the SEAL Brotherhood? Find out when CALL TO HONOR *by* New York Times *bestselling author Tawny Weber, goes on sale in February 2017.*

Turn your love of reading into rewards you'll love with
Harlequin My Rewards